WRITE UP

POETRY AND PROSE ANTHOLOGY

BY

RETFORD WRITERS' GROUP

Retford Writers' Group

Some of these pieces have previously appeared on the website,
www. retwords.wordpress.com
where 500 more pieces can be viewed.

Copyright © 2023 remains with the individual writers

Picture copyright is ascribed,
Otherwise it belongs to the writer.

Edited by Kevin Murphy

Published by

The Lime Press
1 Lime Grove
Retford
DN22 7YH

INTRODUCTION

Retford Writers' Group has met fortnightly since 2011, even during Covid, when permitted, in gardens and gazebos.

Aspiring writers come together in the library to share pieces of writing of every sort, in a good balance of poetry and prose, fact and fiction, to get and to give constructive criticism.

Over 500 pieces have been shared on the web, at https://**retwords**.wordpress.com/ some of which appear in *Write Up*. This is a second Anthology following 2018's *All the Write Pieces.*

The individual writers have edited their own words. I have simply gathered them together in book form.

As we aspire, we hope we perhaps inspire you to take up pen and paper or finger to screen, to give new life to your thoughts and ideas.

Kevin P Murphy
Published as Kevan Pooler
Editor

Retford Writers' Group

CONTENTS

How to read a Poem by Andrew Bell	1
Family Watch by Frank Carter	3
Anyone seen them? By Nick Purkiss	8
A retelling of the story of Bucephalus by Sue Scrini	10
Digging Down the Days by David R Graham	13
WEIGHT WATCHERS by Joan Saxby	18
My brief encounter with the Queen by Nev Wheeler OBE	21
Amanda and the Black Book by Patricia Graham	24
Holidays by Rachel Hilton	27
WAR by Patricia Graham	28
School Memories by Rachel Hilton	29
Time Flies by Michael Keeble	32
CONNECTION by Samantha Richardson	36
Connected by Chitose Uchida	37
Gloria's Gold BY John Holmes	38
IN THE DISTANCE by Barrie Purnell	44
WORDS by Joan Saxby	46
FOLDING by Daniel Toyne	47
Letting Go by Cheryll Richardson	48
Saucy Dream Comes True by Nick Purkiss	49
Millennium Tapping by Chitose Uchida	51
CAN PRAYER BE THE ANSWER? By Barrie Purnell	53
Bedtime stories by Andrew Bell	55

WRITE UP

Truth behind 'Knick-Knack Paddywhack' by Kevin Murphy	57
Shadows by Cheryll Richardson	60
STRESS & LINKS by Daniel Toyne	62
Grief is the Price we pay for Love By Peter Brammer	63
WAR By Rachel Hilton	64
WHAT IS A BOOK? By Samantha Richardson	65
Shock by Kevin Murphy	66
THINGS THAT I FOUND by David R Graham	67
The Last Tram by Frank Carter	69
TAKING UMBRAGE by Daniel Toyne	74
An online World by Sue Scrini	75
Our Ukrainians - 75th Anniversary by Kevin Murphy	77
Mr Verity by Andrew Bell	80
STUCK INSIDE OF RETFORD by Barrie Purnell	82
WATER IN THE BLOOD by David R Graham	86
Shape of Water by Chitose Uchida	91
THE RICHNESS OF POVERTY by Joan Saxby	92
The Picture on the Wall by Frank Carter	93
THE BLUE HOUR by Samantha Richardson	98
A dream come true? By Sue Scrini	100
About the Writers	103

Retford Writers' Group

WRITE UP

Retford Writers' Group

How to read a Poem by Andrew Bell

I suggest you take a poem
and hold it to the light.
Then feel it's presence,
as you do when you walk
into your first home
or into a holy place.

Does it have a pleasing shape?
Does its coach work
have any flaws or scratches?

Do the lines speak
to each other
in manageable slices?

Try walking inside it and go
into the rooms.
Let it speak to you.
Ask it to tell you it's name.

Is the diction good?
Does it have a pleasing tone?
What about the choice
of words?
Would you be happy
if they were left
within reach of children
or displayed in a public place?

Is it too wordy?
Watch out for this,
for in all your poems
you will find that less is more.

Now look beneath the surface.
Is it telling a story?
How is it coming over?
Do you need more time?

Are there any dark corners
that warrant further exploration?

Many poems are quite happy
to be taken at face value.
They may be there to entertain you.

But you will find others that carry
layers of meaning,
calling you to unpeel them.

So what do you do?
Ask yourself: is the poem worth
further exploration?
You may decide to try again
and find there is nothing
there, or be tempted
to tie it to a post
to extract a confession.

Better then to pause and reflect
or failing that, to step outside,
take some fresh air
and go on your way.

WRITE UP

Family Watch by Frank Carter

I am sitting where they usually sit me. It's one of those chill-warm September mornings when chestnuts fall, birds assemble with a weather eye and the village Jeremiahs come out to lament another English summer. There's Mother who's done me up in pink organza to match my sisters …. mm, well maybe. I suppose she means well, but so long as she feels she is in control, I can be left in peace … And there's Pops trying to be calm and unflustered and achieving the exact opposite.
It is the morning of Charlie's wedding.

Fanny comes bouncing downstairs, to be greeted by an exasperated Pops: 'Where on earth is Adele?'

'She was awake, Pops, when I got up. I've just this minute been into her again and do you know what she said ….'What time is it?!'

'God help us! Do we have to nanny that girl?'

'I told her, Pops: 'Time you bloody-well got up!'

On cue, Adele materialises at the top of the stairs. Good old Adele. 'Morning everyone,' she chirrups then flits off into the bathroom for an hour or two.

'And didn't you say that ... that new, young curate chappie is calling this morning?'

'He will be here, Pops, and he's Father Benedictus; please do try to remember.'

'Why's he coming now anyway? He won't be needed until the service. Bet he doesn't ...'

'He will be here. I promise.'

A car comes crunching to a halt on the gravel path at the front of the house and we hear voices whooping and laughing. Everybody is *so* jolly this morning. It is Aunt Sophie with her new man. We all liked the old one; Jerry was fun to have around. But this new creature is a Mummy's Boy, all teeth and oily hands and fawning over Aunt Sophie. Adele says he is all flannel and soap, keeping Sophie immaculate and smelling of lavender.

I feel a hand on my shoulder. It's my Pops. He rolls his eyes to the skies, tuts and knows exactly what I am thinking, he says. He eases me to one side and clambers into the drinks cabinet, emerging with a bottle of Johnnie Walker and two - only two – glasses.

'Morning Sophe! Looking bewitch…. erm ….charming as ever. Like the frock. How are we Nigel? Join me in a toast? Drink the health of the bride-and-groom-to-be, eh?'

Nigel is slithering in my direction but happily is diverted by Pops' offer. He says he feels compelled to accept …. but has to have water with his whisky. Of course we all know: he is wetter than a duck's bottom already. Aunt Sophie and Mother go through their standard routine: right cheek to right cheek, left cheek to left cheek, vacuous smiling and 'dahling this, dahling that'.

It's now I notice Fanny being slightly removed from all this family palaver. Her eyes are filling up. She turns and runs upstairs just as Adele emerges from the bathroom. They appear to collide, look long at each other and then …. fall into each other's arms! From where I am sitting, it seems Fanny is being comforted by Adele. Who would have thought it!? Sensible, grown-up Fanny being big-sistered by the frivolous, irresponsible Adele! Whatever is happening!? The whole family will be leaning on *me* next. Naturally I want to know what's got into Fanny. But that will have to wait. The pair of them disappear into Fanny's room, closing the door with a bang.

Everyone who's anyone, and is here, vanishes post haste to the drawing room, where drinks are the order of the day. Mother tells her guests that I'll keep a look-out for late arrivals, which she knows suits me. I have told her that I am not happy to be dressed up like a prawn cocktail.

'Nonsense, dahling,' she says and flounces off to inflict her charms on somebody else.

Fanny and Adele emerge - unseen, except by me. Each heaving a large bag, a hold-all, which they proceed to lumber down the back stairs to the conservatory door. They see me and Fanny puts a finger to her lips. I am allowed to see, apparently, but say nothing.

And Father Benedictus is here. I haven't seen him coming but when he heads straight for my sisters, he is clearly not come to rehearse either the happy couple or his homily. Looks like a man on a mission. He nods in my direction. 'Janet', I think he calls me, and probably knowing at once he has my name wrong ... focuses his attention on the job in hand.

And the job in hand is ... to pack both cases into the back of his ancient Citroen.

Fanny reappears and not in her pink bridesmaid's creation ... but in jeans and sweater. Adele stands. Stands and stares. And I am watching. All I can do.

Fanny has something quiet to say to Adele who gawps and wipes her eyes, then to me: 'Love you.'

What can I say?

Father Benedictus takes Fanny's arm and hoists her into the passenger seat. The pair of them drive off. Fanny and Father Benedictus. I have to say that again. The curate and Fanny, my sister, Charlie and Veronica's bridesmaid for the day, drive off together.

Back at the assembled mob, where I am reintroduced, Adele commandeers attention. 'Everybody,' she calls, 'I have a pronouncement.' I'm sure she means 'announcement' but what the ... And with a stage-presence and self-control I didn't know she possessed, Adele informs the congregation that there has been a change of plan. Father Benedictus has been called away on diocesan business but Adele is sure we will find 'a substitute'.

A few eyebrows are raised and I hear 'Oh dear' and 'Well now' but nobody seems too surprised. Adele makes no mention of Fanny. Mother, however, feels the need to reclaim the limelight and prepares her dying swan routine. But here comes Pops to the rescue: 'Let's call Anfield 'Arry; he'll always oblige if there's a drink in it.'

There being no flaw in the plan, everyone picks up the conversation where they left off and Pops duly returns, saying Canon Hargreaves, known to all good parishioners as Anfield 'Arry – he's been a season-ticket holder since the Shankly era - is happy to oblige an old friend – and can he watch Match of the Day later? The Canon is the retired vicar of the parish, who delights in being wanted - so long as, like Pops says, his glass is never empty.

No-one else turns up; no-one else disappears. Canon Hargreaves comes; he sees, imbibes and conquers, and most importantly, most people would say, he marries Charlie and Veronica with due ceremony.

The wedding goes off surprisingly well.

Charlie and Veronica say the right things more or less at the right times. The best man tries his lamentable best. But he's a Bertie Wooster reincarnation, who refers to the new Mrs Charlie as 'a fine young filly'. Whereupon, the Drones in attendance roar their approval and the filly in question blushes from her forelock to her fetlocks and gives Charlie her darkest 'just you wait' look.

No-one is obviously rude or drunk.

The Canon approves of everything, especially Mrs Barton and what she is nearly wearing.

My parents are still talking to each other at the end of the day.

The speeches are mercifully short, the vol-au-vents and sandwiches tolerably tasty and the champagne plentiful – which is the main thing. Well, almost the main thing. The fact is that we two bridesmaids steal the show. Our guests are pleasantly surprised and say so. Usually I am just a fly on the wall in this household, but I find myself being quite decent company for once. I mean, not exactly mingling, not socialising, but not embarrassing either. Adele is, as usual, lovely to look at and more than that, she is being the perfect hostess, putting guests at their ease, filling glasses, engaging everyone in the celebrations.

And now a whole year later, their first anniversary and all is well. Today is another of these warm-chill September days. The woods have turned gold and tawny red, Canada geese are taking to the skies and Mr Phelps' arthritic hip is the village news. The house is still once more. Mother dear is busy-bodying around. Pops is in his den.

I am sitting where they usually sit me.

And I do often wonder what became of Fanny and Father Benedictus.

Picture Wikipedia Commons

Anyone seen them? By Nick Purkiss

Anyone seen my glasses?
Came the familiar refrain.
And we knew mum's spectacles
Were missing once again.

The search became frantic
Amid fears they might be lost.
Found them in the microwave,
Five minutes on defrost.

Anyone seen the remote?
Dad shouted out madly,
The Chase is on in a minute
I don't want to miss Bradley.

Drawers opened, cushions thrown,
We searched down every seat.
It turned up in the fridge
Between cheeses and cold meat.

Anyone seen the keys?
Son was borrowing the car.
Without means of ignition
He wouldn't travel far.

Trousers shaken, jackets checked,
He feared another night in
But eventually they surfaced
Deep in the recycling bin,

WRITE UP

Anyone seen the charger?
This place is such a pit!
Daughter desperate to know
If she'd scored a TikTok hit.

She stomped and cursed,
Turning out every pocket.
In fury, failing to see
She'd left it in the socket.

Anyone seen Grandpa?
He was here a while ago.
We searched house and garden
But still he didn't show.

He's always here by one
Waiting to be fed.
Then we heard him knocking
Locked inside the shed.

Missing glasses by Aaron Hammond

A retelling of the story of Bucephalus by Sue Scrini

The dealer was not quite concealing his nervousness as the young prince inspected his horses. Alexander, charged by his father, King Philip to select the best war horses for the army gazed impassively at the circling animals. The day was losing its heat as shadows lengthened over the training field at the edge of the barracks. A few soldiers lounged in the shade, polishing weapons or cooking their evening rations. The air was heavy with the smell of wood smoke.

The dealer, like all of his ilk, was engaged in listing the attributes of the animals. Alexander blocked out the stream of unlikely claims of their talents. He was well aware that a comment or joke often served to distract a potential buyer from observing a fault or weakness so he kept his gaze on the horses.

To be fair to the dealer, these animals were quality. Bred in the rich grasslands of Thessaly, they were sturdy, well muscled and in top condition. He checked for any signs of ill health. There were no snotty noses or weepy eyes. Even though you would expect some to be nervous their droppings looked good - no runny shit. They walked out well, no hint of lameness. So far so good.

He nodded to his horse master to call up the riders to test how well trained the horses were. They brought out their blankets and strapped them onto the animals' backs. Most of the horse were already wearing bridles. The horse master moved along the line fitting bridles to the others. Most accepted the bit easily. Just one of the animals seemed to be playing up. Alexander had mentally selected him for his own. Taller and more powerful than the others, he stood out from the herd with his proud bearing. He had the same air about him as the best bull in his father's herd of cattle. Alexander thought he'd call him Bucephalus or bull-head if he bought him. If the horse showed as much spirit when ridden he'd make a fine mount for the leader of the army. Now he showed that spirit with his tossing head but eventually two of the grooms managed to fasten the bridle.

Alexander preferred to watch just two or three horses at a time as they were put through their paces. The first group all looked good and he signalled to the horse master to have them taken to the horse lines. Out of the next group, one was moving a bit short, a sign of possible lameness in the future. He was rejected and given back to the care of dealer's groom.

As the selection process continued, Alexander noticed that his riders were avoiding the difficult horse. They'd been chatting earlier with the men in charge of the dealer's horses. Some snippet of information had been passed on which was deterring these confident horsemen from riding him.

Alexander could sense the dealer's discomfort as the number of untested horses dwindled and only Bucephalus was left.

He was led forwards, a groom on each side of his head, which was an ominous sign in itself. A rider reluctantly came forward out of the group and vaulted onto the horse's back. As he sat up, the grooms stepped back, the horse took two stilted steps forward, arched his back and bucked. The rider was too experienced to fall off at the first buck, but as soon as the horse's hooves touched the earth he sprang up again, twisting in the air, head between his knees and landing with a jarring rigidity. The man was soon on his back on the dusty soil. The horse stood sweating and trembling but allowed the grooms to catch hold of his bridle. Someone in the lines guffawed. Alexander's glare cut the sound in half.

The dealer started gabbling something about the horse:" never done it before, must have been stung by a wasp", but his voice trailed off into silence as Alexander turned the glare onto him.

"I'll take them, including this one." His horse master was clearly appalled: "But sir..." He began.

Alexander turned to the dealer. "The price of the other horses will be as we negotiated. The price for this one will reflect the fact that he is clearly unrideable. It will be your safe passage from here. Think yourself lucky that I haven't had you whipped for your attempt to defraud me."

Over the next few days, Alexander spent every spare moment with Bucephalus, winning his trust. He thought he knew the reason for the bucking, but he couldn't afford to look a fool in front of the men so the time was well spent. He gently rubbed his hands around the horse's head and ears until he accepted the bridle willingly. He placed his riding blanket over the animal's back, sliding it this way and that until the horse was used to the feel of it on his sides. Then he called for a large chest to be brought to the stables. He had Bucephalus led out to stand beside the chest and then stepped up onto it. The horse immediately tensed up, his ears back. The groom took a firmer hold of the bridle but Alexander told him to let the horse move away if he wanted. Again and again, they repeated the exercise until Bucephalus accepted the sight of Alexander looming above him.

The day came for the final test. Alexander decided it would be in the heat of the early afternoon when the men and horses would be sleepy. The smaller the audience the better. He had Bucephalus led out to the exercise ground. He vaulted onto his back, but stayed low, leaning over the horse's neck.

He told the groom to lead the horse forward, he could feel Bucephalus was taking easy relaxed strides and so gradually straightened and raised himself upright. Bucephalus' ears flicked back. His stride shortened. Alexander, hardly breathing, murmured to him and stroked his neck. To his relief he felt the tension leave the horse's back muscles. He quietly instructed the groom to step back and rode around the perimeter of the exercise ground.

As he urged the horse forward to a trot and a canter he became aware of his men gathering to watch and applaud the spectacle of the great Alexander who had tamed the untameable horse.

Digging Down the Days by David R Graham

'Colm?'

'Are you just trying that out, or are you after getting my attention?'

'I'm after getting your attention.'

'I commend the brevity of your approach. Are you wanting to ask me something, or tell me something?'

'I'm wanting to tell you something.'

'Alright then, but before you do, to avoid any adverse reaction on my part, in a public place, do you assure me that what you are about to tell me has nothing whatsoever to do with any madcap theory about Time?'

'I do.'

'Noting that hesitant expression in your eyes, I venture to ask what it is you are going to tell me?'

'I am going to write a book.'

'Are you?'

'What do you think?'

'I think I'm glad I wasn't drinking when you said that.'

'What do you mean by that?'

'I mean, writing a book. Do you think you would be up to such a time-consum…do you think you would be up to such a task.'

'I gather from your tone that you don't think I am?'

'Far be it from me to utter discouraging words, but I confess to a sizable degree of scepticism.'

'Why is that?'

'I've seen what you do with your tongue when you're filling out betting slips.'

'There's nothing wrong with sticking out your tongue when you're writing. It aids concentration.'

'I don't doubt that, but writing a book will take a lot longer than filling out a few betting slips on a Thursday morning. Such a monumental undertaking could take months or even years. If your tongue is sticking out all that time, you might not get it back in again. An affliction that would pose a serious speech impediment. Not to mention a potentially embarrassing obstacle to drinking. And then there's the real possibility that if you look at someone, they might think you are taking the micky.'

'I am confident I can keep my tongue where it belongs.'

'Assuming that you can. What will it be about?'

'What?'

'The book you will be writing.'

'It will be about our lives as navvies.'

'When you say, our lives. You mean you and I?'

'I do.'

'Noting my doubtful expression, how do you propose to go about that?'

'I will start off where we were born. The families and that. Then where we went to school. Friends and teacher and the like. Then our first jobs. Earning money and going out and things. And girls. And then proceed from there to the present day.'

'That's over sixty years.'

'It is.'

'It will be a big book then. Long.'

'It will.'

'Have you seen the inside of a book recently?'

'I had a look at one or two in the library.'

'Did you note that they generally have lots of pages? Hundreds in some cases, with thousands of words on them.'

'I did.'

'And you are aware that a book covering sixty years of our lives will require an awful lot of writing?'

'I expect it will.'

'Do you think you are up to the task?'

'I do.'

'How do you propose to do it?'

'What do you mean?'

'I mean, I know you can't tell the difference between a computer and a breadboard, so will you be writing the book by hand? Using pen and paper.'

'I expect so.'

'A doubtful tone there. Given the length of such a book, how many pages will you write a day?'

'A day. Jesus, Colm. I don't know.'

'Uncertainty there. So, let's be generous, and say you will write two pages a day. And since such a lengthy book would probably contain three or four hundred pages. You would be writing for at least two hundred days. Probably more, given your lack of experience.'

'I expect so.'

'A lack lustre tone there. But let's suppose, for a moment, that you commenced such a task. On what day would you be doing the writing?'

'What do you mean?'

'I mean, you wouldn't want to be doing it today. Today is for drinking, right?'

'Right.'

'Tomorrow's Friday. So, we will be getting over today.'

'We will.'

'And the weekend is for the dogs and the football. With a bit more drinking in the evening.'

'It is.'

'What about the Monday?'

'Do a couple of pages of writing on a Monday. I don't think I could do that, Colm. It would be no way to start the week.'

'It would not. And Tuesday's Bingo and Dominoes. So that's out.'

'Wednesday is lunch and cards at St Albina's.'

'Thursday, we're back here. So there doesn't seem to be a day free for the writing.'

'There does not.'

'What about writing in the evenings?'

'In the evenings. I don't think I could manage that, Colm. There's the Sky Sports to catch up on. There's the supper to be had. And then there's the medical routine for getting ready for bed. That's a tricky one. No, trying to do two pages of writing of an evening would be a serious distraction.'

'Could you write in bed?'

'Write in bed. That would be terrible awkward, Colm. I would need a table. No, I couldn't manage the writing in bed.'

'Okay then. Let's leave that there for the moment. For argument's sake, let's say you could find the time to write a couple of pages a day. What are you going to call the book?'

'Digging Down the Days.'

'Really?'

'That's a working title. I'm thinking we could work on it together.'

'Are you?'

'I am.'

'A rising note of enthusiasm there. So, you want me to help you expose my life in black and white, for all the world to read. In a book written by you?'

'You won't be exposed. I'm not going to use our real names. I'll make up names for us. And use a different name for myself. A pen name, it's called.'

'What names are you going to use for us?'

'I was thinking I could be Frank. And you could be Terry.'

'I don't think I would want to be called Terry, in a book about myself.'

'Why not?'

'I've been Colm for a long time now. I've grown used to the name. I would find it difficult reading about someone called Terry if he's supposed to be me.'

'It wouldn't be you, though. It would be a character.'

'You said the book will be about us. You and me. How will I know I'm reading about myself, if I'm reading about someone called Terry, knowing that I am Colm?'

'But you would not have to think about yourself. You would just read about what Terry or Frank, or whatever name you want, did over the last sixty years.'

'He would be doing what I did, wouldn't he? Living my life.'
'He would.'
'So, I would be reading about Terry, or whoever, living sixty years of my life?'
'You would.'
'That would be a very unsettling experience.'
'Why would it?'
'I might not like the fella.'
'What's not to like? He wouldn't be real.'
'Sure, that's even worse.'
'Why is it?'
'A fella called Terry, who I might not like, who's not real, living sixty years of my life.'
'But you would really be reading about you. He would be you. You like yourself, don't you?'
'Not if I'm called Terry, I don't.'
'I don't understand that.'
'Of course, you don't.'
'What's that supposed to mean?'
'It means that I don't think that you have the academic gumption needed to write a book.'
'Neither do you.'
'Granted. But then neither do I have a fanciful mind.'
'A fanciful mind. Is that what you think I have?'
'Based on your catalogue of past fantasies, I do, yes. And you must admit that the notion of you writing a book is a prime product of your fanciful mi…'
'Do you know what, Colm?'
'What?'
'Feck the book. And feck you, too. Ye hoo'r.'
'Hoo'r is it.'
'Oi! You two! Sit down! If I have to tell you again! I'll throw the book at the pair of you!'

End.

WEIGHT WATCHERS by Joan Saxby

When one attends the Weight Watchers
You have to line up in a queue.
They eye you up like vultures
And then ask "What did you do?"

They ask "Have you been on the biscuits?"
You say, "I had but a few.
I also had chicken drumsticks.
Thought that was the right thing to do."

They shake their heads and frown at you,
And tell you, "You must try harder."
They say "Drink water, lay off the vino
And don't go in into the larder.

Eat more lettuce and go play tennis,
And never ever sit down.
Go to the gym, don't drink Guinness
And take a walk into town.

Learn to dance, take a trip to France
Try to chew on frogs' legs.
Whatever you do, don't take a chance
You must stop eating up dregs.

If you don't do what we tell you to,
You'll never get any thinner.
 Whatever you do, don't eat stew.
We want you to be a winner.

Eat less bread, dilute the spread
And keep off the herbs and spices
Cut out the white and eat brown bread
And don't have too many slices.

WRITE UP

Learn to love prunes and eat more greens
And think how they live on the Med.
It's really not as bad as it seems,
And learn to go early to bed.

Be ever so good, don't eat a pudd,
It will be on your hips by morning.
You'll stay awake, so be really good
Or you'll listen to Hubbie snoring.

Try not to sin, give up the gin
It's not very good for you.
You're better with water, and we think you oughta
Never eat vindaloo.

Don't lick your lips, take tiny sips
And don't eat too much sugar.
If you fancy fruit, just suck on the pips
I know it's a bit of a bugger.

Don't eat chocolate, it flies to the bust.
You'll regret it if you do.
Take all the icing off the cake,
 And throw it down the loo.

Never hide some crisps in a drawer,
Eat water biscuits, be careful with dips.
Always suck your soup through a straw
Count your calories, never eat chips.

Do the right thing and don't learn to cook
Instead dance like John Travolta.
Throw away your recipe book
Instead do the rumba and salsa.

Jump up and down, thus you'll get thinner
You'll take an inch off your hips.
If you really want to be thinner
Squeeze a lemon through taught lips.

Don't eat gravy, go join the Navy
And help them to raise the flag.
Scrub the deck when the sea's all wavy
Do this and your boobs won't sag.

Never, never put sauce on things,
Especially if you're not sure.
Don't open the fridge for things.
Be firm and slam the door.

Swim a mile before breakfast, learn to hurdle
You'll lose three inches and more.
This will help you to tighten your girdle,
So make it your Weight Watcher's Law.

When you attend we'll measure your hips,
I'm sure you know the score.
Don't go home and eat fish and chips
Next week you might not get through the door.

Learn to love a celery top,
Try not to lick the trifle dish,
Soon you'll be able to shop at Top Shop
If you scrape the batter off your fish.

Think of England, and double the sex
You'll be thin like Posh
And fit like Becks
And very soon you'll fit in those frocks.

Show concern and you'll have no ills,
And learn to look after your heart.
If you don't you'll have to stay on the pills
So promise us that you'll start.

Try to think thin, don't raid the bread bin,
And take a good book to bed.
Remember these rules and don't give in
It's better than being dead.

WRITE UP

My brief encounter with the Queen
by Nev Wheeler OBE

From Angela Grant, Nev's Daughter:

Here is the poem,' My Brief encounter with the Queen', and written below a bit of background for your information. Dad loved going to both the Library poetry cafe and The Writers group for what, unfortunately turned out to be his short time here in Retford.
Dad came to Retford to stay last January because of a fall at the Independent Living flats where he lived in Sheffield. He sadly passed away on 19th August but had made the most of his time in Retford, attending the poetry cafe and writer's group and since his retirement from being a head teacher in Sheffield where he had lived all his life he had returned to his former hobbies of art and writing, in particular writing poems.

The first poetry cafe he attended in Retford was on the subject of Kings and Queens, so Dad wrote a poem about his experience when he went to Buckingham Palace to meet the Queen and receive his OBE for Services to Education. He was nominated for the award by the parents, staff and Governors of the School, Intake Primary School where he had been head teacher for many years. We finally managed to persuade him to retire at the age of 73 in 2006 when he was the country's oldest head teacher.

Nev Wheeler, Nev Wheeler, where have you been?
I've been down to London to see the Queen.
Nev Wheeler, Nev Wheeler, what did you like best?
When the Queen was pinning a medal on my chest.
But the funniest was right at the start,
When a Lieutenant Colonel in the Guards
Taught us the Royal Protocol of how to bow or curtsey
Resplendent in his uniform, bright red tunic,
White jodhpurs black knee length riding boots and spurs.
He then demonstrated 'for His' and 'for Hers'.
To the men, Don't do a 'Sir Walter Raleigh' bow
with a flourish from the waist.

Just look ahead and bow your head,
but not with any haste.

Then he turned to the ladies, teaching them to curtsey
in all his Guards officers uniform he did a perfect curtsey.
He never laughed or even smiled, neither did we,
at what looked like an unreal fantasy.
But watching him was Darcy Bussell the famous ballerina
I don't know if he'd seen her.

Graceful movement being a speciality of hers
but she never once let her face slip
as she was given an unexpected curtsey tip,
from a uniformed Guards officer wearing boots and spurs.
We then formed a queue, no not for the loo,
But to enter the Royal Ballroom to music from
The Band of the Grenadier Guards.

Her Majesty was already there to give out all the awards.
Finally my name was called and I walked towards the Queen.
She pinned the medal on my chest.
We then shook hands and I gave her hand a squeeze
Then, by starting a conversation, she put me at ease
and this was the Head of the United Kingdom
and all the Commonwealth nations.
Talking to me and about my work in education.

The citation for my medal was 'For my
Services to education in Sheffield.
She had been well briefed and speaking to me
In such a friendly manner yet having an
amazing quality of retaining Royal demeanour.
My brief encounter seemed much longer
and my admiration for Her Majesty was growing stronger
By the minute, in my brief encounter.

WRITE UP

Nev Wheeler, Nev Wheeler where exactly have you been?
To Buckingham Palace receiving an OBE from the Queen.
Nev Wheeler, Nev Wheeler you must be very proud.
I feel so proud, I could shout out loud!
But not just about the medal, the OBE
But the handshake and the interest in me, that day,
In that brief conversation that seems like only yesterday.
I am so proud of my city, Sheffield and the education there.
I am so proud of my country with traditions everywhere.
I am so proud of the Queen and her remarkable reign.
'God Bless the Queen' and now 'God Bless the King'
'King Charles and Queen Camilla, long may you reign'.
As you embrace the new roles recently invested in you.
I'm confident you'll serve our country well, as those before
Setting the highest standards for those who follow on,
So God Bless all your family, each and every one.
Following the traditions that make Great Britain great.
God Bless our country – Great, Great Britain.

Nev Wheeler OBE

Amanda and the Black Book by Patricia Graham

Amanda walked slowly towards the Regency green front door of a 1970s detached house. The hedges at the side of the garden path were overgrown and weeds were appearing between the cracks in the concrete, indicating a lack of care and love for the property.

Many weeks had passed since the death of Amanda's father. A man who seemed to prefer seclusion, devoid of any interest other than his stamp collection. Amanda hadn't had a close relationship with her father, neither of them being very affectionate towards each other, only visiting him when she felt she had to.

On this particular day, a very wet and cold one, Amanda had arrived at the house with the dreaded thought of having to empty its contents so that it could be put on the property market for sale. She had never liked the house, even as a child. She remembered her mother being vibrant, so much energy, always adventurous but never being able to fulfil her dreams because of a husband who feared his own shadow.

Amanda turned the key in the Yale lock and opened the door to reveal a dark, dusty hallway with a pile of letters on the floor waiting to be opened and placed neatly on the hall table as her father used to do. Letters that would be answered promptly and precisely to avoid any delay or misunderstanding to the sender. Letters that would take the place of play with Amanda and her sister. Any excuse to avoid interacting with them and enjoying life.

At the age of 16 Amanda moved out of the family home to live with her mother's sister. She was so caring, loving and a lot of fun, just like her mother, but with no partner to hinder her. Amanda loved her Aunt almost as much as her mother. Now and then, Amanda would spend time with her Aunt and mother, times she remembered with extreme fondness and happiness. Amanda smiled as she picked up a photograph from the hall table of her mother smiling with her and her sister giggling on their mother's lap. How her heart ached for those days to return but the pain of her mother's sudden death brought a black cloud over her happy memories.

As Amanda trod on the first step of the stairs, she shuddered at the thought of emptying and cleaning her father's bedroom, but it had to be done, and as her sister was living abroad it was left to her to complete the task alone. Her husband had to work that day and her children were in school.

As she opened the bedroom door the musty smell hit her nostrils, a reminder of how long it had been since she had entered this room since her father had died. There was a sense of guilt, but not grief, in her heart at the way she felt; nothing, absolutely nothing.

As Amanda made her way to the bedside cabinet she noticed a black book which had slipped behind the wooden headboard of her father's bed. She managed to retrieve it and on opening it she thought it would probably be full of old stamps, but as she turned the first and second pages, she realised that it was a diary dated a year before her father's death.

At first she wanted to dismiss it but she recognised her father's handwriting. Should she read any of it, wasn't it meant to be private? She went to put the black book into the top draw of the bedside cabinet but curiosity rose up in her mind and she began to read the elegant handwriting.

Saturday, 26th June 2010: Amanda came to stay for a few days after the sudden death of her mother. What a delight it is for me when Amanda visits, reminding me so much of her mother – vibrant, full of energy and adventurous. How I wish I had let her mother be who she really wanted to be, instead of being afraid of losing her in her enthusiasm to experience life outside the walls of this house.

Sunday, 27th June 2010: Amanda made lunch today, my favourite, kippers, mashed potato and peas. She does everything to please me, but I just can't, just can't bring myself to tell her what a lovely daughter she is. I feel trapped in this frightened, anxious state, unable to express how I really feel. I did try once, to reach out and take hold of Amanda's hand, but she moved away, not wanting to get close.

Monday, 28th June 2010: I waved Amanda goodbye this morning. I was sorry to see her leave. It was lovely to have her company for a couple of days. I hope she doesn't leave it too long before visiting again. I wish I had told her I loved her. I can't write any more, the tears are blurring my vision.

Amanda closed the black book because from the depths of her feelings tears had risen, burning, hot tears recalling those few days spent with her father, wanting to talk about her mother but not wanting to show her emotions to her father. Now it was too late. She would never be able to share her feelings with him.

After spending some time clearing her father's bedroom, she picked up the black book and held it to her chest, wanting to experience the emotions written on the pages by her father. She placed the black book in her bag and decided it would be the one thing she would keep from her father's life.

Her heart ached for her father, but as Amanda closed the front door to the house, knowing it would be the last time she stepped inside it, she decided that she would focus on her husband and two children. She would cook her husband his favourite meal, kippers, mashed potato, and peas, and let the children choose what they wanted to do for the weekend. She decided she would tell them how important they are to her and how much she loves them.

Holidays by Rachel Hilton

I went on holiday to Paris, with my boyfriend, he proposed.
Unfortunately, he ran away, when my MS was diagnosed.

The first time I went abroad, it was a family holiday to Spain.
And all it did the whole damn time, was pour it down with rain
.
We went last minute to Gran Canaria, and boy that was fun,
I wanted to explore the island, all he wanted to do was drink in the sun.

I hopped on a plane to meet a chap in USA,
He returned home with me, what more can I say?

It's great to travel, there is so much to see.
But I'm always happy to come home and have a cup of tea.

WAR by Patricia Graham

Artillery crashes into my space
Lashings of cruelty disturb my life
The petrified faces of the innocent I see
Will this never end?

My world is full of noise,
Men shouting, gun fire booming above my head
Women and children screaming, running
No peace, no calm, hopelessness surrounds me.

Where is my child, where is my child?
The sound of despair in my ears
Blood sweating from the brow
I've never seen such outpouring of fear.

How peaceful this land used to be
Shopping, music, laughing, being free!
Now darkness and grey smoke-filled air are the norm
What future can war possibly bring?

But, it is twilight I see
Flowers, trees, and buildings tall
Breathing in bomb free fresh air

Ah, I shall dream of peace, tranquility
And the enemy shall fall.

London 1943 No license history

School Memories
by Rachel Hilton

School days are meant to be the best days of your life.
I beg to differ.
When I first started school, I didn't enjoy the lessons.
I missed my mum, I didn't like long days away from her.
As I became more accustomed to it, it wasn't so bad.
My teacher, Mrs Willis, was lovely,
A lot of the children accidentally called her mum.
My mum taught me to read before I went to school,
I loved reading and absorbed any fictional books.
But then we moved, again and again.
Dad was in the Air Force; I was a RAF brat.
Every time I started to feel settled, we moved,
Which meant another new school, again making new friends.
At one point we moved off the RAF base,
My parents bought a new house in Leeds, we were going to finally settle down.
No more moving house, no more living like nomads!
I can only say I had been sheltered,
In smaller village schools, with fewer children,
Two or three smaller classes in each year.
Suddenly, I was at what felt to me, a huge school.
It was a middle school, with four years,
And five large classes in each year.
With moving so much I didn't have an accent,
The other children picked up on it.
I was bullied for being a snob, for being soft, for being shy,
For not understanding what they were saying.

I was in the first year, completely overawed,
I kept myself to myself, not mixing much.
I was put with a girl, to show me around the school,
The standard for the new kid.
It was around that time I realised I wasn't going to be the new kid ever again.
Or so I thought.

Continued on at the middle school,
Then moved onto the local high school, with all the other children,
With my friends.
At 14, we chose our options, for our two-year GCSE courses.
I loved English, language and literature, and Drama.
I knew what I wanted to be,
I wanted to be a secondary school English and Drama teacher.
I chose my options, after long discussions with my English teacher,
I wanted his input, to help me with my longer-term choices,
For his thoughts about the appropriate A Levels necessary,
The qualifications I required to then go to University.
I was excited, I knew what I wanted to do.

Then the bombshell was dropped.
We were moving when my dad left the Air Force.
I was gutted, my plans, my ideas, all gone.
My parents bought another new house,
And that was our move underway.
Another new start,
More bullying because I was the new kid,
I was shy, I had a funny accent,
And also, because my parents owned a new house, on the big estate.
I was bullied by the other teenagers, by both boys and girls,
Even those in different years to me!
It all came to a head when I was pushed down some stairs,
And knocked unconscious, all due to the lies of another student.
And the headmaster did sweet fuck all. He wanted it kept quiet.
Nobody was disciplined, even though I knew exactly who had pushed me.

A lot of my schoolwork had been lost due to the move,
It was never received by the new school,
I was only told when it was too late to do anything about it.
I knew there and then, I was fucked.
I knew I did not want to stay on into sixth form at this school.
I knew my GCSE results were going to be shit.
I knew I could not stay at that school; I did not feel safe.

All my plans for my future were out the window.
When I said I was leaving school, my parents weren't happy.
I had made up my mind, I was never going to step foot in that shit hole again.
The bullying had occurred, I felt victimised, and the headmaster did nothing.
How in the hell could I be expected to go back there?
Unfortunately, there was one aspect nobody ever mentioned.
I could have gone to college, studied GCSEs and A-levels.
Then gone onto university.
I had been led to believe that colleges only offered vocational subjects,
Such as hairdressing and childcare, but not GCSEs and A-levels.
I was terribly disappointed when I found this out, but it was too late.
I had already left school.
Six schools in 12 years are not a good basis for a decent schooling.

Rachel Hilton

Time Flies by Michael Keeble

I was born on 16th June 1922 when George V was on the throne. He was the current Queen's grandfather. I was 14 when he died and his eldest son Edward V111 briefly sat on the throne, but was never crowned. I remember that my Dad thought he was a waste of breath, but my Mum thought he was wonderful. As it turned out, it seems that he was a bit of a fan of Herr Hitler, so perhaps my Dad was right. Fortunately, his brother, George VI, was not so susceptible to the sort of flattery that Mr Hitler handed out and agreed with Mr Churchill that we should never surrender.

The way it was then, even though I had had very good results from my exams, there was no thought of sending a girl to university. I left school at 14 and went to college to learn shorthand and typing. My Dad was working in the Inland Revenue at the time and, as I had very good speeds in shorthand and typing, he found me a job there. So, by the time war was declared I was 17 and already working as a secretary in the Inland Revenue.

When war broke out, we were sent to Llandudno in Wales which was safer than staying in London during the blitz. Life there was very peaceful and as a seventeen year old I was not short of admirers among the soldiers that came to the town. My friends and I would go to the dance halls where we danced until we dropped. Later in the war, the Americans came to town. They had money and were much more fun than the British boys.

I tried not to get too fond of any of the soldiers because they were about to go to fight in the war, and I had heard about too many girls who had lost sweethearts, but one tall handsome American soldier won my heart early in 1944. I had been dancing for a while and was sitting this one out when this tall man came up to me and, very politely, introduced himself as Bill and asked if he could have the next dance. He was so polite and so different from the British Tommies that I accepted willingly. He really knew how to dance, not only the traditional dances that we were used to, but also dances like the jitterbug. From the moment I met him, he was the only boy I wanted to step out with. He went away in the spring and, apart from one letter from him at Christmas, I didn't hear from him at all after that. My Dad told me to try to forget him. He said that he would have gone back home to America and would be resuming his life there. I found it easier to believe that than to think that he had been killed. Anyway, I learned to stop thinking about him.

We moved back to London soon after the war and lived in a nice semi-detached house in a quiet street in Harrow near the Metropolitan Line. I soon made new girlfriends and started to go out to the local dances again. I loved dancing. This one night I had gone out with my friend Ruth and was dancing with a lad when out of the corner of my eye I thought I saw Bill. Perhaps I hadn't managed to get him out of my mind after all. My dance partner spun me round and I shook off the thought. The dance finished and I thanked my partner and went over to sit with Ruth. We were chatting to each other when I became aware of someone standing in front of me. I looked around and there was Bill and he was asking me politely if he could have the next dance. I flung my arms around him, and we danced till the end of the evening. We were married later that year. It was 1946 and I was 24 years old.

Bill had been demobbed in November 1945 and had come back to the UK to find me. He had asked around in Llandudno and the Inland Revenue. All he found out was that I had moved to Harrow, but he did not know the address. He began to visit all the dance halls in the hope that he might find me and then that night he thought he had spotted me on the dancefloor. He was afraid that I had not remembered him, and he was very nervous when he asked me to dance. It was a relief to him when I flung my arms around him.

We visited his parents in New York, then came back to England where we set up home in Retford in Nottinghamshire. My Dad helped Bill set up as a builder and after a couple of years of hard work the business was thriving. Our son Alan was born in 1948 and our daughter Lucy in 1951. Bill was still working all hours, so didn't get to see the children much in the early years.

As the business prospered, we moved to a bigger house in a little village to the north of Retford. All too soon the children left home, firstly for university and then to pursue their respective careers in Advertising (Alan) and engineering (Lucy).

Lucy was first to be married in 1975 and produced Jasmine, our first grandchild, in 1978. In 1980 Iain was born.

1980 was a big year for us, as not only did we now have a second grandchild, but this was the year that Alan introduced us to his friend James. He had told us that he would be visiting and that he was bringing a friend, so it was not a surprise when he turned up at the door with James in tow. What was quite surprising was the way he sat us all down in the kitchen with a cup of tea and explained that he and James were moving in together.

I had long suspected that Alan was homosexual (or gay as they like to say now) but had kept my own council. I was afraid that Bill, who was very much a man's man, would find it difficult to cope with. In fact, Bill seemed nonplussed by the whole thing and said "Oh that's nice, that will help with the mortgage" or something like that. Following his lead, I said "I'm pleased for you both. I hope it works out for you" and we carried on chatting in a normal way. I liked James. He was a quiet, polite, and very good-looking young man.

Later that night when we were alone, I asked Bill if he understood what Alan had meant. "Of course I did" he said, "They are going to live together". "But did you understand that that meant they were lovers" I said. He was silent for a long, long time, and I wasn't sure if I should say anything more. After an age he said "No, that's OK. If he is happy, then I am happy". I gave him the biggest hug!

Sadly in 1985 Lucy split up from her husband (I never did like him and even now I won't mention his name) and came to live with us with the grandchildren. Iain and Jasmine are lovely children, but they took a bit of time to settle in with us. They both went to the village school and at first they struggled to make friends. Lucy found a job with a small engineering firm in Gainsborough designing and making packaging machines so the children were with us at the end of school and during the school holidays. I now understand why people have their children when they are young!

Alan and James married in 2014 and are very happy together. Both are retired now and spend a lot of time doing charity work. The grandchildren followed the same path as their mother and went to university. They are bright children and both went to Cambridge.

Jasmine is very active in politics and Iain is a lawyer. They are very busy, and I don't see much of them. They have their own lives to live. Lucy had moved out of our house with the children in 1995 when she was made a director of the packaging company. She moved into a nice house in the village, so I still see a lot of her. She is now semi-retired and a non-executive director.

Bill died on 11th September 2001. He had been dozing in front of the TV in the lounge. I remember coming in with a cup of tea for him. The TV was showing live coverage of what we now know as the 9/11 horror. Bill appeared to be asleep. I put his tea down on the coffee table and stared with disbelieving eyes at the scenes on the TV, gradually coming to realise that this was not a film but was happening in real life. Bill was New York City born and bred and I will never know whether the realisation of what was happening broke him or it was simply his time.

I tried to stay in our house for as long as I could, but although I had lots of visitors, I was lonely. After a year or two, I agreed to sell the house and move in with Lucy. She converted a barn which she had in her garden, and I moved in there. It has made a very happy home for me.

It is strange watching one's children getting older. Alan is almost completely bald. Lucy's hair has turned a fine white like my own. Even the grandchildren are going grey. Oh, I forgot to say, I have four great grandchildren and a great great grandchild on the way. It is my hundredth birthday this year and the children are planning some big event to celebrate.

As I sit watching the Platinum Jubilee events taking place for the Queen (my fourth monarch if you count that idiot Edward) I cannot help but reflect on the way things have changed and how much I have seen.

I am tired though. Perhaps I will be able to sleep when I have given the family my hundredth birthday to celebrate.

Picture BBC News Olmedia

CONNECTION by Samantha Richardson

I dreamt of the demise of humanity,
An exit from all sense and sanity.
The rise of A.I. and a cashless society,
The reliance on a power source and the lack of propriety.

All our transactions and conversations tracked,
Self-service checkouts and accounts hacked.
Our map reading ability entirely zapped,
By SATNAV and trackers, our every move mapped.

In the cloud and the machines that store our souls,
The keyboard warriors and the obsessive trolls.
The words on a screen unable to debate,
A difference in opinion and a desire to hate.

An end to human connection in this technological world,
No face-to-face contact, our minds swirled,
With brain washed messages and deepfake pics,
With A.I. art and Neuralink brain chips.

I dread the day when all this implodes,
No power, no net and the world explodes.
There is no plan B, no going back,
For human connection, back on track.

Connected by Chitose Uchida

Deep Deep Down in the soil
Roots of trees are entangled
Just like our blood vessels

Talking
Chatting
Gossiping

Deep Deep Down in our brain
Synapses are entwined
Just like tree roots

Talking
Chatting
Gossiping

Deep Deep Out Into space
Stars are intertwined
Just like our synapses

Talking
Chatting
Whispering

Deep Deep Out In space
Spirits are connected
We All are connected

Talking
Chatting

Being

Gloria's Gold

The opening of the comic novel **by John Holmes**:

(Soccer-mad college graduate Gloria grapples with her parents' issues and online 'catfish' at home in Orange County CA, while across the ocean a wealthy English aristocrat embraces the green cause)

'Yeah, we crushed it.' Gloria was on the phone, glancing across the table at her friend Annalisa. The two soccer crazy twenty-two-year-olds were at The Flying Loon coffee shop in Irvine and it was her dad calling.

'And the score?'

'Yeah, 5-2. Annalisa sent off.' She moved her legs to avoid the kick. Most people saw Gloria as a serious-minded social science graduate and ardent supporter of charities, but Annalisa ('Ant') could bring out her more playful side.

'Really?' her father said. 'Mr. Garcia will be mad over that. Oh dear. Still won, though. That's the main—'

'Actually, it was me got sent off.' Ant's shoe had connected.

'Oh God, Gloria. Remember—' He sounded agitated.

'Just kidding, Dad. They were a dirty team but I scored one – and made the others.'

'Oh good. That's my girl.' He chuckled happily. 'What about Annalisa?'

'Got two. They were just her usual easy tap-ins, though. Mine was twenty yards. Goal of the season.'

'It was a frickin' pass, you liar!' Ant exclaimed. 'You mishit. You fell over. It hit the goalie's ass and rolled in!'

Another kick from her landed, this time on the shin. 'Ouch!'

After the call: 'Glo, why do you tease your dad so much?'

'I don't. It's just so rare we get to have a laugh together these days.'

'But doesn't he have a heart condition?'

'No.'

'You said he did.'

'Did I? No, I didn't.'

'Well, he will if you keep talking like that.' As Gloria took a sip of her honey cinnamon latte, she looked at her friend for a moment: almond eyes, neat bangs, long black hair tied back. Slighter than her. Less dark, prettier. No, less pretty.

'Not my dad,' she said, smiling. 'He'll live to a hundred and three.'

Gloria's drive back to Mission Viejo in her blue Toyota Camry usually took twenty minutes, but there was a jackknifed rig on the 405 freeway and she was forced to take a detour.

She started thinking about her dad Frank and the last game he'd attended. She was desperate to impress him but nothing was working for her team the Hummingbirds that day. In a rare raid into the opposition's penalty area, she detected the softest touch from a defender's boot on her right foot and tumbled over theatrically. She was immediately booked for diving and her father's frustration blew out of control. He shouted angry abuse at the referee, accusing him of taking bribes. Red in the face and still protesting, he was forcibly ejected from the ground. She was substituted, the team lost 4-0, the coach was later fired, and Gloria resolved never to cheat again. Father and daughter travelled home in shame and silence that day. Fortunately, there were no highway obstructions to prolong the torment. After that he reluctantly decided it was wiser that he not attend, for the sake of his health.

When Gloria pulled up on the white gravel drive at the Spanish colonial villa on the edge of town, 'Timeless' Ray (the laziest gardener in all Orange County, according to her mother) raised his heavy head and gave her his customary wave. The arrival of the tall, athletic Latina in her navy tracksuit was an excuse for him to pause from the pretence of work and simply admire. He adored Gloria as did pretty much everyone else except for the opposition on match days. To Gloria, Ray represented calm authority, though not one she would ever wish to rely on.

Frank was upstairs in his office, his long legs stretched out under the large empty desk, on a transatlantic Skype call. He was talking, or rather mainly listening, to old Layne, ostensibly a lord or baronet or some such. It was never clear to Gloria what he was; all she knew was that her dad was always on Skype with him. Layne was forever moaning about his situation, solitary and absurdly wealthy in his scary-looking gothic mansion deep in the English countryside. She could never understand why her dad even wanted to indulge him; Frank was always upbeat, Layne unremittingly negative.

She decided to listen for a while because the Englishman's posh accent amused her:

'In America and other, ahem, enlightened places, wealth is revered. But in this pisspot of a country I'm marooned in, it's despised. It means a few rich people can be loathed and envied by everyone else, blamed for everything, and most importantly, be required to pay for everything. Every tub-thumping halfwit wants this persecuted minority to give up all they've got in tax so the government can go and waste it.'

'I'm with you on that, Layne, although I think over here people both love and hate the rich.'

'I already pay more tax in a year than most people earn.'

'I can imagine you do.'

'Indeed, I could easily build a hospital with what I pay in a year's tax. In fact, I do. I build hospitals all over the world through my charitable foundations.'

'That must be a lot, for sure.'

'But, as you're aware, selfless charitable work is only part of what I do. I also have to manage my properties.'

'Of course you do.'

'Some people think management is just sitting on your arse and swanning about.'

'That's mean.'

'Well, as you know yourself, it *is* sitting on your arse and swanning about, but thinking and planning and organising as well.'

'Of course it is.'

'Or half-listening to someone you've paid to do all that for you, who's passed it to someone else who's not even half-bothered.'

'I'm sure that's right.'

Gloria had heard enough of the old fool for now. She wondered whether her father liked him because he helped him appreciate that his own life was not so lousy. Hearing Layne bleating despite all his riches was to her a fine illustration of how, once you'd reached a certain level of physical comfort, your mental wellbeing no longer depended on how much wealth you possessed.

She checked the morning's Facebook messages. There were three new friend requests: two creepy-looking guys from out-of-state and a coach from a rival soccer team. She accepted none of the requests.

She'd also received a direct message: 'Tough game today but what a brilliant goal! Well done!' She felt gratified.

'Didn't I tell you we could do it?' she exclaimed out loud. After seventy-five minutes of evading trips and wild tackles she'd had the best possible reward. Annalisa had been correct, however. Everyone was expecting Gloria to pass, but her foot slipped as she struck the ball which then flew high and with force straight into the far corner of the goal, beating the 'keeper who could only flap at it in frustration.

But who was it who was so quick to compliment her? She looked at the name. It was not of anyone she knew. The picture was of a forty-year-old woman who was supposedly local.

'Weird,' she said aloud. 'Sketchy, for sure.' She closed her Facebook page and listened to see whether her father's Skype call with his English aristocrat friend had ended.

They hadn't finished. For a few moments she sat following the conversation.

Layne was still carping about the burden of being wealthy, sounding like he might croak at any moment:

'Lately I've come to realise the right to accumulate wealth is a fortress that must be defended at all costs,' he said.

'Not literally, I hope,' Frank replied.

'Of course not. The way I see it, wealth must be allowed to evolve. It's organic. It's the most natural thing in the world. That's why trying to destroy it always fails in the end.'

'It does.'

'And you can have your high-minded socialists spreading the gravy about the way they do, but they soon create their own elites and *they* certainly know how to help themselves, thank you.'

'I can see that.'

'It's very stressful for us. You see, there's no one you can talk to. You can't phone up a support line – "Can you help me, I'm a multi-millionaire?" – and you can't trust anyone because they're all after your money. It's the loneliest job in the world, I tell you. And worse than that, everyone secretly hates you. I ask you, Frank: who would feel sympathy for a depressed rich man?'

'A maybe not-so-rich woman?'

'It's so unfair, what with all I do for charity and to help fight climate change.'

'It is.'

Layne gave a heavy sigh. 'But I'll just keep plugging away at my projects to keep me out of trouble.'

'Projects?'

'Animal projects. You know, I told you before: rewilding the estate with beavers, European bison, sand lizards on specially made dunes. All sorts.'

Gloria closed her door. Rewilding could wait.

Online, she noticed Trey had sent her a message. He was in Las Vegas and was telling her he'd already won three thousand dollars on the slot machines that morning. He'd been a friend until she discovered, from a routine check, that he wasn't who he claimed to be. According to his Facebook page he was twenty-three, but his real age was thirty, and he was not living in Vegas permanently as he claimed but Wisconsin. Gloria had also established that his Facebook picture was not of him but of a male model living in Malmö, Sweden and that he was not a 'sought-after music producer' but a sales assistant at Plumbing Parts Plus, and his real name wasn't even Trey. He said he was keen for her to fly out to Vegas 'so we can be together as one at last', and he would even pay for her ticket. She did not believe a word of it and replied that she had a conference to attend in San Diego, adding, with the twist of an imaginary knife, that she did not feel he was 'fully committed' to her yet.

Gloria left her laptop to check whether her father had finished his call with Layne. Opening her door, she heard nothing and so went to see him. 'How's the rewilding going?' she said facetiously.

He shook his head. 'Beavers and bison,' he sighed. 'Oh, I don't know.'

'Why do you even talk to him? Is it because he's a lord or something? What does he even want?'

'I met him at some environmental business event.'

'What's environmental business? Sounds like garbage collection.'

He gave her a helpless look. 'I mean, green. A green conference.' He sighed. 'Is the interrogation over?'

'So defensive! You sounded like his therapist just now.'

'Gloria, please. He's just a friend. I am allowed friends.'

She realised she'd perhaps gone too far but then said, 'I worry about you.'

'Well, don't.'

She returned to her room. She had no desire to hound him, only to help. Of course, he resented the very idea that he might benefit from her help.

GLORIA'S GOLD

John Holmes

Out Now   *Daisybluepublishing.com*

IN THE DISTANCE by Barrie Purnell

From a distance we look into a future
Which cannot know tomorrow,
All we see are those neglected sacred fields
That hold our monuments to sorrow.

From a distance we merge into humanity
Knowing no two people are the same,
Only getting closer can we see the difference,
And difference sets the rules of the game.

From a distance we ignore other's problems,
Walk away our conscience clear,
But in our hearts we know we would be kinder
If those in trouble were standing here.

From a distance it's so easy to be brave
Sometimes we find it safer to be blind,
A few have the strength to be heroes,
But moral courage is much harder to find.

From a distance everyone may seem happy,
Looking more content with life than you,
But from a distance you just can't see the cracks
Their happiness is leaking through.

From a distance don't judge anyone until
You can see behind the mask they wear,
So you can see the frown hidden by the smile
And see the hurt that lies behind the tear.

From a distance it may seem that friend of yours
Is happy to be where they stand,
But looking closer you may find they're waiting
For you to offer a helping hand.

From a distance we look back to those we loved
Retrieving their lost love from our hearts,
We add their love to all that we have now
Welcoming the comfort it imparts.

From a distance no one can tell you love them
Don't delay, go and hold them close,
Let your lips deliver them your message
They're the one you love the most.

From a distance I travel to those held dear
To be closer to those I need,
With these words I put my arms around them
Knowing for me their love is guaranteed.

From a distance that brave marble monument
Looks no different from a headstone on a grave,
Who knows if God is in the same confusion
Over who is to be damned and who'll be saved?

From a distance I may still look quite young
Just an image your mind's created,
As I come closer with your eyes wide open,
You'll see I've simply been backdated.

From a distance I can see the gates of Eden,
The good people already safe inside,
Me, I'm still a long way from redemption,
But at least I can always say I tried.

Retford Writers' Group

WORDS by Joan Saxby

Words, words, words
They can fascinate or titillate or hurt you through and through
But if you love someone so much, hurt you must not do.

They can praise, advise and harmonize
And help you through hard times
But you must never use them as offence that's in disguise.

Words can be effective, emotive and free lance
But should not be used unkindly
So put this out of bounds.

They can be colloquial, foreign or in brogue
But they should never ever be
In a hurtful mode.

They can be corrective, instructive or directive
But always use them wisely
Never too objective.

Use them as a smoothing iron
But never as a whip
For they can be uplifting or cut you to the quick.

Words can be quite playful
Humorous or gay
But always be quite mindful and be careful what you say.

In other words don't lose hem
Never be without
 And always use them wisely and never ever shout.

FOLDING by Daniel Toyne

I remembered this morning morning's mantle
More my Mother's than Elias'
Blowing airing shaking folding
From a line aligned to the bicameral lawn's diagonal
A hypotenuse sowing growing part strawberry bed
Part bedding plants rhubarb and late biennials

Memory like dice cast on paper or on pressed cotton
Depressed caressed from languid past forgotten
To future unwritten by-passing today
Always the delay the might the may the unforgiven
A touch a torch a thought a doubt unshriven
All stains remain now done they shun the only-Begotten

A fledgling gardener clambering mundane rockery
Familial mockery shattered crockery of tension
Invention inversion and by extension the re-invention
A version mulled milled by actors singers now enactors
Shake break take unlimited rows of factors
A lupin petal moment calls stalls mimosa-yellow roses

All details sound inbound despite the past now found
In momentary calls fresh fabric smells the bells
Of churches of parents now both under ground
The plummet-sound of wind in oaks in birches
A stream a dream of laundry growth combing both
The bend the rend they always send in countless searches.

Letting Go by Cheryll Richardson

I'm learning the art of letting things go
I'm learning how to go with the flow
I'm learning about the power of 'now'
My ego subsumed in this physical realm
A feeling that angels are now at the helm

Becoming 'detached' from all cumbersome labels
To rise up and finally becoming enabled
To be free of those shackles
From those ties that
have bound
My head and my hands
My mind only on shifting sands

My child's heart intact
The giant within coming to the fore
Allowing, believing I can be so much more
Than I ever thought possible
Raising my game
Stepping up and stepping out
To greet challenges with courage and conviction
I am safely on the path towards 'home'
In this beautiful journey of life.

Saucy Dream Comes True by Nick Purkiss

It was the applause, always the applause. Every night when Jonathan closed his eyes, he could see and hear his adoring audience showing their appreciation for another triumphant performance. Women of a certain age would lose all inhibition in making their affection clear. Their partners would clap and nod knowingly in recognition of his enviable appeal to the fairer sex. Even children would squeal with excitement, their faces red from laughter at his effortless hilarity.

It had been that way ever since his perfectly timed 'Baa' as second sheep from the left in the Year 2 nativity. It had earned a spontaneous standing ovation – well, his mum had leapt to her feet in the front row, clapping and blowing kisses in his direction. This caused one of the kings to forget which gift he was proffering before promptly bursting into tears and making a hasty and tearful exit in the direction of the boys' toilets.

Undeterred by the 'silly over-reaction' of the boys' parents and head teacher, his doting mum was more convinced than ever he was destined to be a star and he was delighted to be indulged. She assured him 'jealousy' was behind his failure to land leading roles in subsequent school productions although even the head had to admit his oak tree portrayal in the Robin Hood panto was unsurpassed in its poise.

Her conspiracy theory gathered momentum when, despite appearing in her hand-made, full Dickensian urchin costume at preliminary readings, he failed to land the role of Dodger in a local production of Oliver! Still, she maintained, Jonathan managed to steal the show as part of Fagin's gang despite being annoyingly obscured from view by the 'awkward big boy' determined to steal his thunder.

A back-street agent begrudgingly agreed to take him on his books when he left drama school with a 'pass' in his diploma but, despite his mum's almost daily badgering by phone or in person for the last five years, he seemed unable to land his big break – until now.

His latest reverie was interrupted by a knock on his door and those magical words – "You're on in five, Jonathan." He'd replayed that phrase in his head thousands of times but now it was reality.

He stood up, straightened his cardigan in the mirror saying to himself, "This is it," and took a deep breath before turning the handle and stepping out.

"The popcorn, crisps and chocolate buttons are on the table, just as you asked, and there's even a bottle of shandy. Curtain up in one minute."

The happy family scene was so familiar to Jonathan from the numerous takes and rehearsals which had prolonged the agony of his wait for his big moment. The actor playing the father was an experienced pro who managed to conceal the undoubted pain from his scalded hand following a domestic mishap on the morning of filming. His bad luck had been Jonathan's good fortune.

The scene unfolded and Jonathan could barely hold the remote control in his sweating hand due to the nervous sense of anticipation. "There!" he shouted and almost leapt in the air as he pressed the pause button with all his might.

He had timed it perfectly. Frozen along the bottom of the screen was the caption 'Spice up your family's meals with our new range of Saucy Sauces'. Above it was the hand, poised with the bottled condiment at the perfect angle to display its eye-catching label. But it wasn't just any hand it was HIS hand, unmistakable due to the scar left when one of his daydreams had caused him to staple himself to the cardboard during an uninspiring craft lesson.

He could barely breathe with excitement as he turned his head to the seat on his left. There, his mother drew a tissue from her apron to dab away her tears of pride and joy before composing herself, looking lovingly at him and pronouncing: "And they said you'd never make it!"

Millennium Tapping by Chitose Uchida

Tap Tap Tap

In 2000 the wet winter made us cry
I arrived on the Finchley Road tube station
People were pushing and shoving
Jubilee Line was closed

Tap Tap Tap

Engineers were standing with a hammer
At the meeting point where the extension met
the original rail
Tap Tap Tap... ...
Engineers were scratching their heads
The width of rail doesn't match
What was wrong?

In 2000 the rain was nonstop
I watched TVnews long in the dust
The landlord's son pulling the radiator off the wall
Millennium Bridge was taped up on the screen

Tap Tap Tap

An engineer was examining the bridge with a hammer
On the swaying bridge
Tap Tap Tap... ...
The Engineer was sighing
The construction was unsafe
What was wrong?

In 2000 the dark winter mornings were misty
I watched TV news in the freezing room
The portable blowing heater was producing meagre warmth
The crash at Hatfield shed people's tears on the news

Tap Tap Tap

Yet again engineers were tapping the metal with a hammer
At the point of the train crash
Tap Tap Tap ... ...
Engineers were shaking their heads
The cause was a lack of communication
What was wrong?

Tap Tap Tap
Tap Tap Tap

"Why is everybody tapping?"
Of course,
Celebrating Millennium!

Tap Tap Tap
Tap Tap Tap

Of course,
Celebrating my jubilant first winter,
Welcome to England!

Millennium Bridge Photo by Sumple - Creative Commons

CAN PRAYER BE THE ANSWER?
by Barrie Purnell

She told me her sorrows in the tracings of her tears,
She loved me with laughter at point-blank range,
But we were merely biding time it appears,
Down to a lonely conclusion she'd prearranged.
I should have seen it coming, but wasn't that smart
That's why I need to know,
Can prayer repair the heart?

Love isn't fair, sometimes it's hard
With moral values only vaguely defined,
Some obligations I chose to disregard,
I drew my own lines to stand behind,
The walls of my virtue porous from the start,
But now I need to know,
Can prayer repair the heart?

I lost myself to love's sideways glances,
Hoping the courage with which I confessed,
And my pleas to the saint of doomed romances,
Would atone for times when I had transgressed.
I regretted the deceptions in which I played a part,
But now I need to know,
Can prayer repair the heart?

I wrote lines to try and quell the rumour,
But my attempted deception was revealed
When she stripped away the humour
From the poisoned arrow they concealed.
I closed the wound but it left its mark,
And now I need to know,
Can prayer repair the heart?

I searched for truth through a fog of illusion
For secrets of souls that rarely get spoken,
I looked for reasons but was never certain,
Despaired that the code could ever be broken.
I mistook love for science, when it was an art,
That's why I need to know,
Can prayer repair the heart?

Love was a language I couldn't translate,
Why couldn't we have kept up the pretence?
My failures just a mix of coincidence and fate,
I was living through the funeral of my innocence,
My timetabled tragedy emerging from the dark,
And now I need to know,
Can prayer repair the heart?

I was lost in love's ever-turning circles
That hang timeless in the sky,
Another casualty of love's reversals
Still no nearer to knowing why.
Knew the destination but couldn't find it on the chart,
So now I need to know,
Can prayer repair the heart?

I built myself a clandestine shrine
For a love that was never dead,
And wrote a book of oblivion rhyme
Full of words that nobody said,
Reached the end of hurt, wanted to restart,
So now I need to know,
Can prayer repair the heart?

I have been whispering in the darkness
Borrowing someone else's prayer,
Holding onto shadows on the floor,
All that's left of the previous affair,
I let her enter my soul, she tore it apart,
Now I am hoping someone will tell me,
Yes, prayer can repair the heart.

Bedtime stories
by Andrew Bell

You say you have heard bad things
about our troubled earth
and it's keeping you awake.
What can I do to allay your fears?

I could tell you another story,
perhaps remind you, now Spring
is here, of that secret kindling of ants
and beetles in the further reaches

of the garden, and all the liveliness
and merriment we found around
the lilacs and the birches.
Or tell you about that time

when a sparrow hawk thumped down
among the hellebores, ripping through
a collared dove, his fearsome eyes,
starlike, flaming gold, fixing me, boasting

his entitlement, as he spread a cloak
around his feast. I could have offered you
a sugar-coated version, but perhaps
I should trust that, in time, you will come

to know how nature really works.
Through the window, I can see the rain
beating against the pane.
You ask if we are in for another flood.

You want to know more: ask why
the sky is so often angry, why, across
the world, they say the trees are rasping
for want of rain.

But there are some things I cannot tell you.
Questions about how humanity has abused
the earth: this shameful legacy
we have fashioned, that now seeks payment.

And, in me, the feelings of guilt: knowing
that I remain a co-conspirator, conniving
in this firestorm of complacency and denial,
looking on, even as the Gods of fire

and water are thrown out of kilter.
All these things you will come to know
when the time is right.
But it is late, and I must leave you to rest.

So let us finish with a prayer and remember
that in the end, it is only love that can heal
the earth. Then I must say goodnight, holding
a picture image of you slipping into sleep.

Andrew Bell

WRITE UP

The truth behind 'Knick-Knack Paddy whack'?

by Kevin Patrick Murphy

The source of the Nursery Rhyme "This is old Man" has been unearthed in the archives of RTE – the Irish Broadcasting Company. It refers to the variety of punishments meted out on the Irish poor during the Great Famine of 1846-53, when a million starved to death and another million were forced to emigrate, despite the fact that the country was a net exporter of food during the whole period.

During the Famine ninety six percent of Irish Land was 'owned' by people who didn't live there – Grandees who had got the land through gift, often through fealty to royalty or chieftains, and felt no allegiance or sense of either ownership or belonging to that land. They lived elsewhere, often in big houses in England, so were 'absentee landlords'. I live in the 'Dukeries' in Nottinghamshire, England, seat of Viscount Galway, whose other titles included Clanricarde, Imanney and Tyaquin in Ireland.

Being absent, they still wanted to profit from their estates of course, either not knowing, or ignoring that they were rotting and stinking through the failure of the staple of the poor in the Potato Blight.

Not that it was Viscount Galway, but this one old man played one merry hell and sent troops to evict people who would not – could not – pay the rent. The playing on the drum could be heard over the hills and sank fear into the very hearts.

Another old man played on two – shoes, leaving a million barefoot children to starve to death.

We know of punishment three which continued into our lifetimes – kneecapping – shooting people's knees to cripple them and be a warning to others to pay up.

Sanction four followed the knock at the door and would be the tearing down of the main house beam and torching.

Punishment five would be setting the hives on the people – a reference to the stinging of whips as they were chased away from their family homes.

Retribution six played upon the few sticks of furniture some of the evicted would still have and the Gombeen men would buy for a bag of meal, or worse, kicking the dog when he's down – not giving him meat – only a bone.

Image - Creative Commons

These punishments have gone into the lexicon of sufferings borne by the people – all the whacks on the 'Paddies', as they became known the world over when they were washed up on foreign shores.

The dead kept the faith and seven took them up to Heaven with number eight knocking on the Pearly Gate.

Finally there is this old man who played nine, he played knick-knack on the spine – a treble pun: knick knacks are small possessions, sold, stolen and burnt; paddywhack is the ligament from the neck and spine of sheep and cattle – a final piece of 'meat' the poor could chew on to stave off hunger; nick-nacks are also the vertebrae used in the famous game of Knucklebones, Fivestones, or Jacks played since even Sophocles attempted to date it. It is played the world over and often used angular bones such as vertebrae. Just as in that other Nursery Rhyme where "The Ring o'Roses" was a symptom of the great plague, he sad reference in this children's nursery rhyme, is to the vertebrae of tens of thousands of unburied children which would continue to be found in fields and ditches around every town or village of Ireland for the next fifty years.

The rhyme for the final verse expresses the fear that the famine would return another year, so the old man, the devil, would play ten and come again.

Each verse concludes to remind all listeners of the greed behind it all – the exploitation of the starving by the rich old man and his venal Gombeen man – living the life *taken* from Riley, and in his drunkenness he came rolling home.

The truly fanciful notion of Kevin "Paddy" Murphy

Shadows by Cheryll Richardson

Come out of the shadows
My darlings, my dears
And so let your light
Shine bright and shine clear

The life you once had
Has now run it's course
No time now
For regret and remorse

A new way forward
Is opening out
A time for those outmoded
Conventions to flout

Your own true colours
Will see light of day
Enfold you surround you
And show you the way

Towards your enlightenment
Nothing to fear
A path of discovery
To all you hold dear

It's easy to slip backwards
Towards darkness and gloom
When surrounded on all sides
By prophets of doom

So walk through the shadows
Yes , pass through the pain
Until you're ripped open
With nothing to gain

Only then in the darkness
Will you begin to awake
The first time in your life
You begin to see straight

So leave the shadows and their secrets far behind

AND

'Let your light so shine before men
That they may see your good works.'

Matthew 5:16

STRESS & LINKS by Daniel Toyne

There is nothing bold, upheld, to bless
In all my memory, reflecting fall.
This call to verse I can address
With links, despairing measure, now recall.
No music of the spheres do I express,
No tyrant acts in violent reign,
Heroic claims I can't confess,
Romantic heights I merely feign.

My life of mediocrity I dress
In layered fabric, from other lives new-dredged.
Against the mono-chromic past I daily press ~
A greater version of myself now pledged ~
And links from past and present, more or less,
In progress, halyard-like, take up the stress.

This piece is constructed to be read either top-down or bottom-up.

GRIEF IS THE PRICE WE PAY FOR LOVE
By Peter Brammer RIP

Peter was our most attending member since formation in 2011.
He died in 2021.
This poem is one of the most visited on our website.

Grief is the price we pay for love,
Leaving memories to treasure,
Heartaches shared by ones who care,
Plus a lifetime's loveand pleasure.

No one knows the pain and hurt,
The loneliness it leaves,
Or understands your simple need,
To be alone and grieve.

To recall those days in happier times,
Full of gaiety and laughter,
When both held hands to say "I Do"
And be happy ever after.

Only time can heal those painful scars,
The scars no one can see,
Wounds so deep they tear the soul,
And will never set you free.

Things come back to haunt you,
A dream in troubled sleep,
A photograph from holidays,
Or a trinket that we keep.

The coolness of those salty tears,
How many can one shed?
Enough to water every flower,
In your favourite flowerbed.

WAR

By Rachel Hilton

displaced families,

hiding in the dangerous ruins,

created by the falling shells,

crying out for their dead.

no one taking responsibility for the atrocity.

a baby unrelentingly cries for his mother,

whilst being carried in a sling by an elder sibling,

unaware of his surroundings,

his bawling falling on deaf ears.

thousands uprooted from their homes,

all thrown into turmoil,

fleeing for their lives.

they have now unwittingly become refugees.

news stories shown around the world,

portraying ordinary citizens,

gunned down in the street,

while queuing for bread.

and still no outraged leaders in the free world.

How can this be allowed to continue?

WHAT IS A BOOK?

By Samantha Richardson

A book is a place where people live.
A place where poets and authors give,
A glimpse far into another world,
A place where hopes and dreams unfurl.

A book is a place where lives are placed,
A glimpse into the psyche of the human race.
Where pictures are painted and anger vented,
Where magical beasts and dragons are centred.

A book is a place where memories go,
Where narratives, a story and characters grow.
A place where philosophy and history give,
An insight into the place we live.

A book is a place where metaphors abound,
Where synonyms and antonyms and symbols are found.
Where murder and intrigue and mystery flow,
Where religion and discussion and arguments go.

A book is a place of understanding and hope.
A place of teaching and desires wrote
On slices of tree, in black and white,
A place where imagination and excitement ignite.

Shock by Kevin Murphy

'Sometimes it isn't a shock,' Jack said, 'bad news and that.'

'Like Chamberlain saying *Peace in our time*, and we all said *is there heck as like!* I replied.

We both laughed. That pleased me. For Jack to have a laugh when he has just received a death sentence. Weeks not months, they said.

He bucked up. 'Hey, we've got to be thankful we've made it long enough to know who the 'ell Chamberlain is!'

He laughed.

Coughed.

Winced.

Wiped his eyes.

He looked at the back of his hand and muttered 'was!'

It's like a slow train coming down the line, I thought. The nightmare of being tied to the line.

We both had it; the discovery; of the lump. Within days of each other, seven years ago. Blood count up. Jaxey - finger up; scans; biopsy.

'It is cancer.'

No, it is not a shock. You have feared it all along.

But that doesn't stop the train; and you are still tied to the track.

Silent movie running through your head. Buster Keaton.

Or Popeye the Sailor Man for goodness' sake.

You can shout for your 'Olive'. I didn't need to, she was there. My Beth. She told me we were alright, the train was on the other track.

We've got time.

Dedicated to Peter Naylor-Morrell, colleague and friend d 3 Oct 2023

THINGS THAT I FOUND by David R Graham

At the wheel of my brand-new Navarre
I set off to circle the globe right around
With the sun on my Ray Bans, I planned to travel afar
Picking up things that I found

I drove down to Dover and onto a ferry
And off again at Calais
I motored through France via Boulogne and Rouen
And continued on through Bordeaux
For Switzerland I was bound
Crossing Austria, Slovenia and Ukraine
Picking up things that I found

I drove across Russia as quick as I could
and stopped at the Bering Sea
With the car on a plane, I made the
Canadian Land bridge
And motored from there to Port Sound
I passed through St John and onto Provost
Picking up things that I found

I made it through Quebec by the breadth of a hair
And crossed the Atlantic by plane
I landed in Dublin and drove to Rosslare
For Fishguard I was bound
From the port at Fishguard I headed up north
Picking up things that I found

At Telford I stopped for a brew
that cost me nearly five pound
Back home that would have paid for two
though I was hungry I did not hang around
I was back on the road after using the loo
At Burton on Trent I stopped for an hour or two
Picking up things that I found

From Burton on Trent I drove at a pace
through Belper, Bolsover and Clowne
From that oddly named place
I was a mere twenty-four miles from my home town
So I stopped to pick up things that I found

From Clowne I motored to Worksop
where fuel was less than two pound.
Whilst I was there I popped into the shop
And picked up some things that I found

https://pictures.dealer.com/b/billynavarrechevroletlakecharles

When I returned to the pump
I was clubbed on my head and fainted without a sound
When I came round my head had a crack
And my brand-new Navarre was nowhere round.
So, alas and alack, having circled the world right around
I have lost all the things that I found.

WRITE UP

The Last Tram by Frank Carter

The boy and his mother sit by the fire in the kitchen. She knits and talks to herself, her face telling him something of what she feels about what she's thinking. He thinks: she is content and she is occupied and not about to pack him off to bed. So he sits quiet, quiet with his two National Geographic magazines, the ones he's found in the attic box that he was allowed to open, the box which belonged to his father, where he kept things from the War. The boy might not be allowed to stay up with his Wizard or Hotspur, but with National Geographics, he can. His mother has said he can look at the magazines, look at the maps, charts and the awesome photographs; and she'll read out what he cannot manage. So long as he's very careful with the magazines; they are older than he is and must be taken special care of. Like this: the pair of them sitting by the fire; both busy with what they like doing. The boy feels his mother is not exasperated with him, just now. Exasperated. The boy has learned the word but does not really know what it is about himself that she finds exasperating. Maybe it's because there's only him and her nowadays. 'You can be so exasperating,' she often says.

The front-door bell rings.
    'Who can that be?' His mother looks up, startled. 'And at this time o' night. You'd better go see who it is and bring them in out of the cold. Don't let the cold in, mind.'
    The boy has been staring fascinated at the Murchison Falls, crocodiles taking wildebeests, the aurora borealis, a solitary bear cub ploughing after its mother over snow-clad Rocky Mountains, another world. His reverie is interrupted. But he likes there being someone at the door.
    He needs no second bidding; off he goes, closing the kitchen door behind him to keep the warm in, he skips down the hallway to the front door. The light from the hall shines through the window pane in the door on to the door step, where stands a familiar figure.
    'Uncle Billy!'
    'Aye, lad, 's me right enough.'
    Uncle Billy is Mr Rae from the terrace next door. 'A wiz jist wantin' tae use yer mither's phone. An' maybe you are just the very lad to use the phone for me.'

'Yes, yes. Come in out of the cold.' Uncle Billy is wearing what he calls his 'auld woolie' and flat cap, both showing signs of snow.

'Naw, lad, I'll bide here an' see the trams pass along. There's the 18 and the 26 keep comin' but she's no back yet. No hame after a' this time. It's snowin' heavy now, gettin' late and she's no hame. No hame yet.'

The boy listens. He feels the cold, the concern, something's wrong. Gone wrong. Going wrong. 'Here's another tram,' he says. Mr Rae steps out of the shelter of the front porch on to the gravel path, the better to see down the drive, down to the High Street where the tram cars pass. This tram stops at the foot of the drive.

But if anyone does get on or get off, the snow keeps that to itself. No-one appears to walk round the corner onto their street …. and up to the doorstep where Mr Rae and the boy are standing. Uncle Billy watches the tram; the boy watches Uncle Billy. No-one.

Only the snow and the trams and the waiting.

'You want the phone, Uncle Billy?'

'Aye, A do that. She's been a' day wi' thon auld crone, Maisie Colquoun. Here's her number; A've written it doon.' He hands a slip of paper to the boy. 'Want you to phone the auld besom and check oot if Mrs Rae has left Largs yet.' He hands the boy a sixpence.

The boy is pleased to help, knowing what Uncle Billy thinks of the telephone. He returns to the hall, closing the front door behind him. Keeps the cold out. The telephone is on the table by the hallstand. He drops Uncle Billy's sixpence into the glass jar by the phone; that's too much, he thinks. But Uncle Billy must be worried. The boy lifts the big, shiny receiver, as he has been taught, and waits.

'Number please?'

The boy checks the slip of paper. 'Largs four-nine-five-o,' he intones. 'Nasty, winter's night,' says the operator. And the boy agrees, feeling very grown up. There's a moment's silence followed by *'brrrr …. brrrr' ….* and again.

Then …. 'Hello, who's this? What do you want?'

'It's me, Mrs Colquoun. Uncle Billy wants to know if Mrs Rae has left you yet.'

'Och, it's just you, is it. You should be in yer bed. Tell that old fool the phone'll no bite. Gettin' a boy to use the phone when …. Aye, she's left a while since; I saw her on to the Glasgow train, the six-minutes-past-seven, like always. She should be home by this time.'

'Thank you. I'll go tell him.'

'Aye and tell him the phone will no bite.'

The line goes dead. He replaces the receiver on its cradle. Babies have cradles. But phones? He is quick to rejoin Uncle Billy, closing the door behind him. He imparts Mrs Colquoun's message - only the train bit.

'Here comes another,' says Uncle Billy. But the tram doesn't stop.

The boy feels Uncle Billy's disappointment; he stands close beside him. Like he does at the rugby, when Mr Rae takes the boy by train to Murrayfield to watch Scotland. Where Uncle Billy joins forces with his old pals from the Borders where he was brought up. Where he and the boy meet Sandy and Jock, farmers from Selkirk, and the Hawick butcher. 'Mind, there'll be no bad language,' Uncle Billy reminds his friends. ' No in front of the boy.' The men nod earnestly. The Hawick butcher looks at the boy, sheepish-like, the boy thinks, and wonders: what language is bad language? French maybe, or Italian?

When yet another tram comes and goes - they hear it before they see it - the boy asks Uncle Billy: has he any tomatoes left? He always helps Uncle Blly plant out his tomatoes from the greenhouse; he'll taste a few, the wee ones; pick out the unwanted shoots and gather the crop, even late into the year.

'Naw, lad, they's a' gone. Mrs Rae pickled the last o' them. Must gie you an' yer mither a jar o' her green tomato chutney. It's real champion.'

'It'll be real champion, right enough,' says the boy, echoing Uncle Billy.

They see the lights of the next tram car though the bare branches of the wood across the street, hear it jolting and juddering up the High Street. Doesn't stop. The boy wants something else to say.

Snow rests on Uncle Billy's garden fence. 'Your fence looks great. You did a grand job there.'

'Aye. we done a grand job, right enough, you and me.'

The boy remembers. He helped, when Uncle Billy was painting his garden fence two Sundays ago. He holds the brushes; when Uncle Billy finishes with the big brush he hands it to the boy who swaps it for the wee brush. Pastor McSween appears. He lives two doors up and is on his way to the Kirk, bible tucked under one arm, sermon smouldering under his collar. He crosses the drive but pauses midway: 'I was just minded to think, Mr Rae, the world would be a far, far better place if some of us would spend as much time worshipping the Lord on the Sabbath, as we do painting our fences.'

Uncle Billy takes the wee brush from the boy, half turns towards Pastor McSween: 'Aye, an' I was jist minded to think, Mr McSween, the world would be a far, far better place if some of us would just mind oor own business.'

It's getting late. The snow thicker, the night colder. The boy has counted three more empty trams. He has an idea: 'Uncle Billy, would you be wantin' a mug of tea?' He feels the man's hand on his head, ruffling his hair: 'Aye, lad, A would that. That'd be just ....'

'Champion,' boy and man say together.

The boy hurries through to the kitchen and into the scullery, closing doors behind him. His mother is counting her stitches. 'Och, you,' she says, 'look what you've made me do.' She restarts: one, two .... five, six .... He notices the time on the mantelpiece: ten-past-ten.

'I'm putting the kettle on,' says the boy, not wanting to exasperate her - again - and tea, he knows, always works.

Uncle Billy has given the boy a mug with his initials on it: BR. Which, he has explained, stands for Billy Rae and not necessarily for British Rail, where he has worked all his life. The boy understands. He boils the kettle on the gas, four rounded teaspoons of tea in the pot, two heaped teaspoons of sugar in the mug marked BR. He doesn't forget his mother, who is pleased to receive a cuppa when her knitting is causing her issues; she smiles at the boy. Then has to start counting again.

He leaves her quickly, quietly and takes careful steps with his full mug of steaming tea through to Uncle Billy. He holds the mug by the handle and reaches out to Uncle Billy, who is squinting through the falling snow. The boy opens his eyes as wide as he can when he is watching, not like Uncle Billy. He tries squinting too. They peer together, eyes straining, wanting and waiting. Mr Rae takes the mug in a large paw and sips his tea. He appears not bothered by the hot or the cold, the boy can tell.

The tea makes its mark.

Uncle Billy sips and sighs, and he looks at the boy, who is watching him, who is with him. 'There'll be no many more trams now. An' see, there's no buses the night, no traffic at a', only the trams.' The boy sees. There is another tram coming though. They see it before they hear anything, all sounds being muffled in the snow. The tram's lights flicker and stutter up the High Street. It ghosts to a stop.

The boy feels something being draped around his shoulders. His mother has left her knitting and her tea and come to the front step. His father's tweed jacket, which has always hung on the hallstand, is wrapped around the boy.

At the bottom of the street something moves.

The curtain of snow parts just enough to reveal a shape. A small figure, slow and deliberate, plods heavily up the pavement, footprints black in the snow, like the tracks of the bear cub, the boy thinks. He feels his heart pump, deep under his father's jacket. Uncle Billy has stepped over into his own garden: 'Aye, well,' he says. The figure has made it to their gate and can be heard chuntering to itself. Uncle Billy has always said: she aye likes to talk.

'A've never been sae fed up in a' ma life.' She rambles on about trains being held up on Fenwick Moor and the freezin' cold and the guard and the night. Uncle Billy intervenes: 'Well, A telt ye.'

He turns towards the boy and his mother, hands over the tea mug: 'Thankee kindly,' he says. 'You have a grand lad there, Missus.' The boy's feet are cold, his hands are cold, his face is cold; inside, he is warm.

Uncle Billy wraps his arm about Mrs Rae, who disappears into his auld woolie. He pushes his own front-door open. 'Come away in,' he says.

TAKING UMBRAGE by Daniel Toyne

Always memory.
Some words remain in the ear and the mouth,
Beyond the Mass and grave inscriptions, beyond echoes
And shadows, preserved in formal English and Italian opera.
A relish. A game giving life to a language called dead.

The Classics classroom, up in the tower, where generations of
Pueri nick-named Dexter, the Latin master, 'sinister'.
Always uniquely, always for the first time.
Words. Uxor, for which I have no need,
Though uxoricide raises questions, possibilities.
Splinters of others ~ regi, patri, fratri ~
Always likely to end in lacrimae.

And other shadows, that stretch in the low equatorial light.
The languages of Empire long gone, wrapped in khaki.
Should I apologise for juggernaut? Or stubbornly stare out
The appropriation of pyjamas and bungalow?
Are reparations required to wash away the shame
Of swastika, the landscape of jungle, trek, beleaguered?

Now, in the language of the young, the savvy,
Lexis is inverted and reversed, leaving the old
To sense in the light of technology and/or inclusion
The shadows of meaning no longer recognised.
An icon is ripped from Liturgy and veneration,
Queer no longer an insult, wicked no longer bad.

WRITE UP

An online World by Sue Scrini

I haven't always felt so sad

With a brain that's like a butterfly.

I think the world is going mad

The internet is one big lie

The yanks are going to vote in Trump

Why on earth would they do that?

Meanwhile I have got the hump

With the bot that fails to chat.

No, I don't need FAQs

Just a person to advise

Oh look there's a bit of news

Into space Galactic flies

Zero gravity's the thing

Their rocket soars above the sky

Down on earth I've seen a link

To something else I want to try.

An app for music to aid sleep

Free trial and then a monthly fee

How easy when I bought to keep

Those discs and records just for me

Another news flash strikes my eye

England's women take the lead

Can't ignore it tho' I try

The little worm's inside my head.

I check my emails once a day

Ha ha I'm sure you guessed! I lie.

With our data we all pay,

No escape e'en though we try.

WRITE UP

Our Ukrainians - 75th Anniversary

An extract from **Convicted for Courage** by Kevin Murphy (published as Kevan Pooler) - a social history of experiences of the WW2 POW camps in Britain.

When Germany invaded Poland in 1939, then pushed further towards Russia in 1943, they recruited captured Ukrainian Poles to join them in the fight 'only against Bolsheviks'. In May 1945 they surrendered to the British and Canadian Allies as The First Ukrainian Army. Stalin wanted 'his' prisoners back - he was executing them - however, by 1947, Britain and Canada gave exile to 8,000 and 70,000 respectively. By Christmas 1948 all the POWs had been sent home and the camps like Colwick, Carburton and Retford's Nether Headon in Notts, were offered as homes to the now EVWs - European Voluntary Workers.

In *Convicted for Courage*, Eric Chapman, himself imprisoned then exiled to Notts for being a Conscientious Objector, befriended the POWs and collected their stories.

The Retford Librarian Josie Husbands of Bridgegate, also supported POWs with books, paper and magazines . Here Eric receives news.

Autumn 1950

I got a somewhat hurried note from Josie Husbands to say she was getting married - did I want to come. Not quite an invitation.

It turns out that Josie has been 'good friends' with the group of Ukrainians, more so with Fedir Walter Wacyk, who gave her an ultimatum: "Jousie, (sic) if you not marry it me this week, I marry it Pat next week." She accepted Walter's gallant offer. He told Mr. Knight, the one-eyed man with a flat cap at Nether Headon Camp gatehouse, who organised the Kommandos (work parties) for NAEC, that he wouldn't be back again. He packed his bags and stayed at a friend's on Sunday.

Retford Writers' Group

On Monday **Fedir Walter Wacyk, married Joselyn Husbands** at St Swithun's Church, Retford across the road from her library and round the corner from her house. Not a very formal affair. Just a few of us and I got the wedding snap.

I can only think that Josie had not considered the notion of marriage, but was struck by it - totally.

At the wedding 'breakfast' slightly upmarket from the last hotel I had visited with Josie, Walter asked me what I actually 'did'.

I told him knife maker, but that I was now a teacher.

Walter has continued using skills taught by a blacksmith while on the run from the POW camp in Italy: he's with Mr Lister the Farrier at Scrooby and is a fully fledged blacksmith now. Josie shared some pictures:

'Walter's *Apprentice Piece* he made to show Jim Lister what he could do. 'It's right beside the Great North Road as it bends through Scrooby,' Josie said patting her man's hand. 'You'll see it every time you come down from Doncaster to Retford. You will come back and see us, won't you?'

I sucked my lips before deciding to mention my metal work experience, but not going back to it because... no I couldn't go back to refusing to make weapons, but I laughed and said I needed him a while ago to sort out my plasher as it had broken trashing the brambles. I had to explain a 'plasher' but oh yes, bring it to him.

Not any more.

The usually fairly restrained Josie actually gushed, 'And look what Walter made me for our wedding present.'

By way of her own introduction to Walter, her lovely husband, she thought I would enjoy his funny English story: when he was brought from the ship in Liverpool over the Pennines to Lodge Moor, the distribution camp in Sheffield, from the window of the bus, Walter gained a warm first impression of the British from the way they treated their 'lunatics'. He saw the men fenced in a spacious field, dressed in lovely white uniforms for their bat and ball game. She raised her eyebrows.

I probably mirrored her, but glumly.

Josie looked to Bella who had a hand over her mouth. She nudged me. 'Cricket, silly!'

I snorted into my drink.

'He saw the cricket game from the back of Mother's house in Retford and he had snorted, too, when I explained to him that the *lunatics* were England's greatest heroes!'

Laughing belatedly, I shook Walter's hand and told l him that I had written up his story mentioning us Grinders and the folding and hammering of metal to make the finest blade.

I now wave to Walter Wacyk the Ukrainian POW's sign as we pass regularly through Scrooby, to visit Palmiro the Italian, Arnold the German and our host, Farmer Alec Fox at Egmanton. Our little League of Nations.

CONVICTED FOR COURAGE

INSIDER EXPERIENCES
WW2 POW CAMPS
IN BRITAIN

KEVAN POOLER

Out Now 100+ photos

Mr Verity by Andrew Bell

A friendly stranger has taken over
the top floor in my head.

A man of culture and refinement,
he wears smart shoes,
with polish well rubbed in;
keeps his best thoughts
in his wardrobe on the shelf
above his suits and ties
and his aspirations,
in other fine pieces,
some suitably distressed.

You will never hear him grumble
about errant thoughts leaking
through distressed tap washers,
embarrassing moments, or missed opportunities.

But, I suspect he has come to teach me,
hold a mirror to my foibles
or, because he never seems to rest,
reset my synapses as I sleep.

More often though, I will find him
playfully disrupting my self-absorption,
like when he sings melodious refrains
through the floorboards above my bed.

At weekends,
I may accompany him in duets,
and sometimes, when I miss a beat,
I can see by his look,
that I'm somewhere else,
reliving those Sunday afternoons,
with the lady I met in the flat below,
the one who keeps my dreams

with her rings in a box.

And when the world is having fits
about this or that,
or when I get caught up
with the problems of mortality
or the properties of dark matter,
or eternity,
or I'm wondering whether writing a poem
is a symptom of insecurity,
he answers my questions
with thoughtfulness and grace.

Then my attic voice
begins to change its tone.
I'll feed on benign spaces
between the words,
put the issues back in their chest,
slip quietly into those silent attic spaces,
and make a cup of tea.

Retford Writers' Group

STUCK INSIDE OF RETFORD by Barrie Purnell

(In homage to Dylan's 'Stuck Inside of Mobile')

He gave me the trigger word
Expecting me to compose
From my imagination
Some poetry or prose,
But there was nothing in my head
The page stayed virgin white,
I would have nothing to present
And nothing to recite.

Oh I'm asking
Can this really be the end,
To be stuck inside of Retford
With the writers' group again?

He said we could write anything
I didn't have to make it rhyme,
But blank verse was beyond me
I just didn't have the time,
The days were slipping past so fast
Thursday's deadline loomed ahead,
I thought I could apologise
And call in sick instead.

I tried to think of happy
But could only think of sad,
I found it hard to separate
The good stuff from the bad,
I tried to embrace Falstaff
But was drawn towards Macbeth,
I tried to think of laughter
While writing words on death.

WRITE UP

Oh I'm asking
Can this really be the end,
To be stuck inside of Retford
With the writers' group again?

I prayed for another lockdown
Or some other late reprieve,
And tried to write a few lines
That would flatter to deceive,
With imagination empty
I resorted to alcohol,
But verses then became obscene
So wouldn't do at all.

I thought if only I could find
An obscure anthology,
Penned by some long-dead writer
Of forgotten poetry,
Possibly just this once I could
Forget copyright applies,
And could cheat a little bit
Maybe just plagiarise.

Oh I'm asking
Can this really be the end,
To be stuck inside of Retford
With the writers' group again?

Every poet is an actor
With the paper as their stage,
Bringing life to all those words
That lie dead on the page,
With every line that's written,
With every stanza that they start,
They give you as a sacrifice
A small piece of their heart.

Retford Writers' Group

I wrote metaphors and similes
Joined by fragmented clauses,
And I tried to make them scan
Using well-constructed pauses,
I called on the god of Larkin
And other poets I have read,
But it was all to no avail
This poet's brain was dead.

Oh I'm asking
Can this really be the end,
To be stuck inside of Retford
With the writers' group again?

I tried to go to sleep that night
But could only dream of this,
I was falling into a lack
Of creativity abyss,
I searched for inspiration
From the late-night radio,
They were talking of the suicide
Of Marilyn Monroe.

Next morning I revert to type
Submerged deep in the gloom
Of a cold and dark November
Rainy, Retford afternoon.
Composing some short verses
About Love and loss and pain,
I found my creativity
Was back with me again.

Oh I'm asking
Can this really be the end,
To be stuck inside of Retford
With the writers' group again?

WRITE UP

I took this as a lesson
For me to stick with what I know,
To avoid Mr. Bojangles
And stick to Desolation Row,
So that is my poem written
'Though I know it's not my best
But what I know for certain is
It'll leave the Writer's Group Depressed

Now I tell you
This really is the end,
I'm stuck in Retford library
With the writers' group again.

WATER IN THE BLOOD by David R Graham

He was a warrior. A fighter. Fearless. Had been since he learned to stand upright: confrontational, combative, offensive. Naturally martial, drawn to a military life, he became a soldier. The perfect outlet for his aggressive nature. Gravitated to special forces. Delta. The tip of the spear. At the apex of his physical and mental fitness. He had no need of politics. No need for family, for friends. He lived to fight. His superiors directed him at their enemies and let him loose. The danger of combat was all he needed to feel alive. Bloodletting fired him. Pain energised him.

He was in pain. Intense pain. His left hip and thigh were in shit state. He had taken shrapnel. At least three pieces embedded in his flesh. He knew it was shrapnel. Had he taken three 7.62 rounds from an AK 47. He would not have a hip or thigh left.

He had heard the distinctive sound of the rounds zinging off Zulu Two's armour as he bailed out of the vehicle. An RPG rocket had flipped the Stryker. It lay on its side. A stricken Rhino. Gutted. The remains of nine operators in its belly.

An IED had blown the lead Stryker, Zulu One to scrapyard junk coated in human remains.

AK rounds came at him like enraged hornets defending their nest. In their buzzing midst he registered his surrounding in stark clarity. No panic. No disorientation. Mud brick hovels rising out of the packed sand that served as a road through what passed as a village. Left. A derelict hovel. Broken down walls.

Rounds tore at his backpack. He knew what that meant. He vaulted a wall, rolled back, stretch full length against its meagre cover.

Incoming rounds from his 4 o'clock. Chewing up the brickwork. Kicking up dust. Sticking to the sweat on his face and neck.

If they had more RPGs. He was screwed.

He was trapped. His back against the wall. His wounds were on fire. The shrapnel was stemming the bleeding. The pain was intense. He sucked it up. The full pouches of his tactical vest were digging into his buttocks and spine. Worst still. His hydration bladder was shot to shit. He sucked on the umbilical anyway.

Rounds struck the wall. Showering him in dust.

Bearing down on nascent panic, he took stock.

His M17 carbine held a magazine of 20 5.56 rounds. He had 4 spare mags. The M9 Beretta holstered to his injured thigh held 15 rounds of 9mm parabellum. He had 4 spare mags. The short-barrelled Sig Sauer in its Velcro chest holster held a ten-round mag of 9mm. He carried 2 spare mags. In addition, he carried 6 barrel-launched MK 13 high explosive anti-personnel grenades. A Blackhawk combat knife was strapped to his ankle. A razor-blade Eagles claw knife was strapped to his left bicep. A pocket on his right thigh held a poly-carbon slingshot and a dozen 12mm steel ball bearings. Used proficiently they could penetrate a human skull.

With two round bursts from his M17 he could take out 60 attackers. If they stood still. If they were ducking and diving, creeping and hiding, he might take out 30. Crippled and trapped as he was, he might take out half that number. The grenades should make them think twice about a full-on assault. Segmented steel wire wrapped around a HE core. They were lethal.

He was lethal. He had serious firepower.

The one thing he didn't have. Was water. Without it for much longer he would be powerless. He was thirsty. His mouth was dry. Early warnings of dehydrating. The release of adrenalin into his bloodstream had increased his heartrate and his breathing. He needed to slow down. Conserve fluids. Water made up 90% of his blood. Without water his blood would slowly solidify. His oxygen supply would drop. His BP would drop. Cautiously, he searched for a pebble. Sucking on one would help to keep his mouth moist. His fingers encountered only hardpacked sand and dust.

The sun was coming up at his 6 o'clock. Through his DBUs he could feel the heat on his legs and groin. Sweat gathered under his kneepads. Morning temperatures were close to freezing. He had dress accordingly. Planning to shed layers as the temperature rose. He could not do that now. His ballistic tactical goggles were protecting his eyes from the sunlight. But they were making his face sweat.

Controlling his breathing he flipped his glove and looked at his watch. 09:23 hours. 37 minutes before the next scheduled comms check with FOB Ripley. 22 klicks southwest of Tarin Kowt. Grid reference 33° 12' 59" N. 69° 32' 10" E. Close on 84 klicks out. 6 hours by road. A Blackhawk could do it in that many minutes. He had no way of calling them in. He was way too far out of range for his personal comms. The GPS phone on Zulu Two might have survived the hit. He would not know for at least 36 minutes. The village was a shithole excuse for human habitation. Primitive. A blip on a map. 30 klicks from Tal'Khak. Grid reference 34° 59' 45" N 67° 59' 01" E.

The inside of his helmet was slick with sweat. He dared not remove it. It was capable of stopping small arms fire and blunting the impact of some high velocity rounds. Beneath his tactical vest his chest was soaked in sweat. Likewise, his armpits, his groin, his lower back. He was bathing in his own body fluids. He had no way of replenishing them.

The firing had stopped. They knew he was trapped. They were probably moving in for the kill. Or capture. They generally did when they were numerically superior. He was not going to let that happen. He hoped they would bring the fight to him. He fed a grenade into the Carbine's underbarrel launcher. He was prepared to die in battle. For a warrior that was a given. He would try to take as many of the enemy with him.

The sun was bearing down on his chest. Like the heat from an open oven. His tactical vest felt as though it had doubled its weight. His carbine was hot through his gloves. Sweat was keeping his eyes moist but affecting his vision. His cheeks and jaw were burning. His lips and mouth were dry. He had run out of saliva. He could no longer control his panting. He used his exposed trigger finger to transfer sweat from his jugular notch to his lips. It tasted of raw salt. Along with other essential elements he was losing sodium. His lips quickly dried.

Exposed to the furnace heat of the sun, he felt his limbs growing increasingly heavy. Losing sensation. If he did not get water very soon. He was going to lose his ability to function. He would be a sitting duck. He could not stay where he was and survive. He had to move. To find shelter from the heat. Even if it cost him his life.

His only option was to get back to Zulu Two. Five metres to his 4 o'clock. Use its meagre cover as shade. Maybe find some water. Maybe find the GPS radio intact.

His left leg was going to be a burden. It was going to hurt like shit when he moved. Crawling was not an option. To slow. He would have to hop skip and jump. It was that. Or die where he lay. Slowly cook in his own juices.

He would move in two rapid stages. Vault over the wall and lie prone. If he got shot up. So be it. Hopefully it would be fatal. If he was still in the game. Up on his right leg. And get to the Stryker as fast as he could.

Getting over the wall was going to be the hard part. He was going to have to sit upright. Place both hands on the wall. And launch his body in one go. He was going to have to move quick. He was going to land on his injured leg. There was no way around that. Chances were that he was going to get shredded by 7.62 rounds as soon as he broke cover. There was shit all he could do about that.

His carbine was going to get in his way when he moved. Braced for income rounds he quickly raised the weapon and dropped it over the wall. Nothing happened. No rounds chewed up his meagre cover. They were either anticipating his next move. Or they had lit out. In the next few seconds. He would know. Gritting his teeth, he sat upright and threw his whole weight over the wall.

He landed on his back. The impact sent a red-hot bolt of pain racing through his injured leg. Without pausing he snatched up his carbine, got his right leg under him, and hopped skipped and jumped to the Stryker.

He made it unscathed.

Had the enemy lit out. Left him for dead. He didn't dwell on it.

Clamping his mouth shut he dragged himself inside the vehicle.

The mangled interior stank of voided body waste and guts. An airborne invitation to a swarm of blow flies. In his desperate need for water, he crawled over the fly-covered remains of his co-operators. Searching their webbing for a water bottle.

He found one. It felt full. He was going to make it after all.

Crouched in foulness and crawling with flies he unscrewed the bottle and raised it to his cracked lips. Even in his shit state he resisted the urge to gulp down the water. His body would immediately reject the very thing it needed.

He drank slowly. Letting the warm water wash round his mouth and moisten his parched throat. When his throat was ready, he drank greedily. His hands shook. A lot of the water ran down his chin and his neck. He slowed his drinking. Lowered the bottle to get his breath.

Something slammed into his back.

He felt an eruption behind his breastplate. Warm liquid flowing down his torso. Over his abdomen. Pooled around his waistband. He tasted it in the back of his throat.

One thing for sure he knew. It wasn't lifegiving water.

Shape of Water by Chitose Uchida

In My Memory
Far Far Far Away

Water in an icy stream
Gushing out purity from the mountain
Water in hot spring
Bubbling out from the earth
Steaming sulphurous odour
Beginning of life

In My Memory
Far Far Far Away

Water on my skin
Pouring down from the stormy sky
Water in my shoes
Burbling and Gurgling
Singing of life

In My Memory
Far Far Far Away

Water in the sea
Grabbing my body away from my father
Green Water in the sea
Cuddling me softly towards the sea bed

No fear
Chatty waves above
Utter peace within me

THE RICHNESS OF POVERTY by Joan Saxby

Do you know how rich you are, though poor
When you can hear and see and feel
And talk but not be found a bore
And with this gift a friendship seal?

When you can feel the wind upon your face
And smell the seaweed on the shore
And with your fellow men keep peace
And be upstanding with the law?

To listen when someone in need
Needs help to understand his world
And you have sown the friendship seed
Though hurtful words at you were hurled?

Don't ever think that you're not whole
For you have riches by the score
The caring that is in your soul
Transcends your poverty and more.

For in your heart there is much love
For those less worthy than you are
These gifts were given from above
Like the guiding light from a star.

WRITE UP

The Picture on the Wall by Frank Carter

My, but it's quiet in here. *Seems there's just me and the picture up there on the wall.* I can hear myself think in here. I can feel my thoughts. Like little fishes they are, come tripping up to the surface and lots of little bubbles pop out. They are mine they are, them little fishes and the bubbles, my thoughts.

Now if you were daft enough to ask him, my George, about pictures and Art Galleries, he'd rip yer head off he would. 'Them places,' he says, 'them's for poofters – waste of tax payers' 'ard-earned cash.' So when I thought I need a bit of peace to clear my head, I thought: where would George least like me to go to think? So here I am in Leeds to give myself a chance to get my thoughts straight.

Now I know you're thinking Leeds isn't going to give me peace and quiet but our Sally came here on a day out from school last year, did the University visit she did. Not that I know what she did but he asked her did she do Elland Road? And Sal said: 'No, we did the University.' And George huffed and puffed: 'Huh! waste of bleeding money.'

And they did dinner in Leeds too, only they called it lunch on account of them being there with Mr Shakespeare; he's their English teacher. And George wanted to know: 'Who's Mister Shakespeare when he's at home?'

'Chap who wrote plays in Elizabethan times,' says Sal.

'Oh,' said George.

Anyroads, in the afternoon they go to the Art Gallery. And that's where I am now.

oOo

I went to see my Mum again yesterday. I don't think she's got long now. My Mum's one of my little fishes, keeps popping up with something to get me thinking. 'Your George,' she says, 'is just like your father. It's taken me until now to realise, but now I'm seeing things as they really are …. the man I married is a bully, always has been all our married life. The man YOU married, Christine, is a bully. Chris love, you know he is. But don't you be like me - like I am now. They've told me I've only got weeks – weeks! Don't be like me now, Christine!'

Don't know what I'll do without my Mum. When I talk, who'll listen? My Mum could have painted the picture on the wall. She knows me better than anyone. It's not a picture of someone, is it? More a ... *a representation of something.*

See, there's a figure and it's muscular but I'm sure it's female, she has my buttocks and her raised arm hides my face – and my intentions. There's a shadow behind her, isn't there? Stooping, self-satisfied, set in his ways, controlling. I'll bet he doesn't know that the raised arm with all her power is raised at him!

I do love George. I hate George. I need George. Do I need George? He is my shadow, he follows my every move. He is the outside of my inside. People see my shadow and don't see me.

Physically, we have been apart for as long as I remember. He doesn't hold my hand, kiss my lips, stroke my back, fondle my hair. But he does want his marital rights he says! Ugh! And that's what he gets – for his manly pride or maybe out of duty to me but not for any reason that matters. Once a week – Thursday - bed - light off. I like to be touched. I want to be touched lovingly. And do I touch him? I do with my obedience, with my roast beef and my apple pie. But lovingly?

My Mum asked me once: 'Did we not love you enough, Christine?' And she reminded me: 'We did have poor Joe to care for; he needed the lion's share; he was in his wheelchair while you were fine and fit. He needed your Dad and me more than you did. And the others, I needed you to help with the others, Christine. And Dad needed you to help me.'

So I was glad when I was wanted. I took George and his fumbling in the dark and his Victorian attitudes and his Catholic guilt. Took him as a promise of things to come. And there have been good times. I have a husband who never misses a day's work, who's given me two wonderful kids and let me get on with the job of bringing them up ... Let me get on, so long as I don't question George and his 'homely routines and simple pleasures' (says he). Good Heavens! he does go on: 'Where's me tea for little me? ... These veg from Carneys? ... This meat from Bob Lamb's?' ... always followed by, 'best butcher meat in all of England.' Every summer holiday is a case of: 'You can book Drakesmere Farm for 't' summer fortnight. Take tha' wet wear. Never rains but pours, down Drakesmere.' Oh dear.

I have never complained because I have never actually felt discontented. I have been happy with the same old routine really. Am I ungrateful, am I taking a risk now when I suggest there has to be more than dreary days and lonely nights? Isn't there more to life?

Not just me that's affected either. Our Andrew cannot get even a word or a look from his father since the lad hit him with the revelation of his sexuality. I am not surprised and indeed welcome the news, since it explains to me a lot about my son. I smile and hold Andrew tight and taste his breath and love him all the more at this minute. But I am hardly prepared for George's onslaught and readiness to 'beat the devil' out of the boy. 'I am not having any son of mine ... I bring the boy up decent and what thanks do I get . I blame you for mamby-pamby-ing him ... I this ... I that ... I ... I ...'

He's twenty-two and old enough to know what he is and what he isn't. Listen to him, George. Listen to yourself, George .... Andrew deserves this from his mother at the very least. But now he has to live away from home.... until he sees sense, George says... or until his mother does.

The picture again. The shadow in the picture does not listen. Just lurks and watches and passes judgments. Whatever you do, whatever you think, whatever you feel, the shadow knows.

My mother dying in hospital, my father going about his usual business, his only worry is where his next meal is coming from. Mum has lived for him and done for him. Cared for all of us – well, up to a point – and if Joe did have the lion's share, Dad commandeered what was left. George? Did I choose George to be a father to me – to be my kind of father?

Sally's view is very different. She declares herself opposed to marriage, pointedly telling her Dad and me that too often marriage enslaves the woman in a dysfunctional lifestyle.

Dysfunctional! Oh George – he erupts but only because he catches the tone of what she is saying; he has no interest in what 'dysfunctional' might mean. Sal doesn't let the subject drop; she says I'm a slave to him - as if I didn't know. Her Dad has already switched off, blaming a University education for his daughter's downfall from his high moral standards. My fault again – for encouraging her to go to University in the first place. I reap what I sow, he likes to tell me … repeatedly.

Mother! I love Sal lecturing me as 'mother'! Mother, you are an intelligent woman (I protest), you should be out living your own life - no listen! – you can be a perfectly good wife and mother and still be YOU. I'm so feeble. Sally says what I say quietly to myself. She speaks out, voluble, confident. The picture is assertive.

I am … at a crossroads.

oOo

Mr Stanley Richardson enters the Alliance and Leicester Building Society. His arrival is a grand event. The American gentleman, we call him. He calls here after his lunch in town on the last Thursday of every other month. I notice and count on his coming, for it is always my desk he comes to. I handle his Account and have done for ten years now. He is my Knight in Shining Armour, or so the girls say, and he greets me SO respectfully, smiles just at me SO … sensually …. thanks me SO sincerely … Mr Richardson. Oh Mr Stanley Richardson, were I Mrs Stanley Richardson …!

The colours are strong and forceful. Streaks of blood red – an angry red. And the background is blue … everywhere blue.

It is OK to dream a little, surely? So what am I? Driven? I need to be strong and I need to please. I do struggle to stand back and take stock and make decisions for ME. It seems I play the same old record over and over. The needle sticks – me too. I am like my Mum, compelled to keep things the same – even if that means we get hurt. What do I really want from this life? I am 45 years of age and what do I dream of? Mr Richardson? Andrew at peace with himself? Sally opening new doors for her and for me? Mum not to suffer any more? Dad just to go away? And George to go with him! But do I dream for ME?

The picture on the wall has become demanding ... overwhelming ... Did I paint it myself?

No!

Oh! I peep round. Did anyone register that that 'No' came from me? Yet, I can leave the Gallery with renewed hope and conviction. My time has come.

oOo

The train back from Leeds runs to time and I find myself contemplating my next move with a sense of …. exhilaration. Like a child off to a party. I know there are one or two things to see to first: George has a Darts match tonight, he'll need his green club shirt …. and they'll want sandwiches ….

Dr Anderson is an unpleasant surprise when I arrive home. And all my little fishes are suddenly nowhere. I just gawp at him and he takes my hand.

'Now, sit down, Mrs Ackroyd, there's nothing to worry about. George has had a slight stroke … he's asleep at the moment … been overdoing it. He's best not disturbed at all. Just try to keep things as they are …'

The picture on the wall is '*Painting* '(1950) by Francis Bacon (1909 -1902). It is in Leeds Art gallery. Detail used.

THE BLUE HOUR by Samantha Richardson

Tim Bamforth Photography.

I hear a solitary blackbird and its melodious call;
The evening stills and the lowering sunlight stains
The house walls pink.

I sit on the steps sipping the potent stuff, as words,
Images and jumbled thoughts try to find a shelf to settle
In my head.

The taint of humanity has left for a while. No-one else watches
The dandelions gather their yellow cloaks
And close for the night, after a day collecting sunshine.
Nor are they watching the gnats scribble their names in the air
Above the birdbath.

The hunk of stale bread I threw out this morning,
Sits quietly in the grass waiting for the robin to come
And gallantly feed his mate.

I absorb this stillness and watch the cloud-wisps form,
Reflecting back the dying of the light, and the dusk
Preparing to birth a new darkness.

How blessed to be motionless and silent in this blue hour,
With no weight of human expectation
Drowning the moment.

The last of the blackbird's song carries off in the fading light,
And my thoughts settle as the stars appear,
Colouring an ink-black-sky with silver,
And sleep begins to beckon.

A dream come true? By Sue Scrini

It has a lot to answer for, that fairy tale.
She's dreaming of a frog prince, changed by a kiss.
Her pinnacle of ambition to attract a male
Happy ever after, ensure a life of bliss.

But, if that handsome prince should be a slimy toad
With poison kiss, all aspects of her life to o'ersee
After she has fallen for his charm overload
Then she realises she is no longer free.

If family and friends dare try to intervene
His childish sulks and raging silence last for days.
The careful bruises are on places never seen
His venom quells her spirit in so many ways.

The irony strikes her only when she's left him
They have a lot to answer for, those brothers Grimm.

Frog Prince by Walter Crane - wikipedia commons

Happy ever after...

MEET THE WRITERS

Andrew Bell had a varied career in legal practice. He is interested in nature, writing pieces for media outlets and teaching, including Philosophy, inspired by spiritual traditions. Andrew's poems have appeared in The Yorkshire Post, The Journal of the Scientific and Medical Network and U3A Newsletters.

Frank Carter was a Psychologist for more than 40 years and having written countless descriptions of people and their behaviour, thinking and feelings in that time, has turned to writing fiction for the past 20 years or so. The fiction, prose or poetry, may borrow from the professional past, or simply reflect an imaginative and curious mind.

Nick Purkiss worked in the regional press as a journalist for 39 years in his native Hertfordshire, then Lincolnshire and Nottinghamshire. After a career as a news reporter, sports reporter and sub-editor, editor and managing editor, he retired in 2022 and is now enjoying the opportunity to write, particularly poems, for pleasure.

Sue Scrini joined the group because she loves reading. She writes for fun and her only previously published work has been the village magazine and letters in various national publications.

David Graham is a founder member of the group. Throughout, he has worked on *Paddy Doran's Box,* 'a bit of Irish blarney' peopled with colourful characters and the situations they create in their pursuit of magical gold coins around County Wicklow in Ireland. Now published as a quartet: *The Fall of Dungragh Hall, Rampere Riot, Leprechauns' Lucre* and *Armed Intruders,* as is a volume of *Short Stories and Poems.*

Joan Saxby worked for the NHS as a Medical Secretary. She now enjoys writing poetry and painting, including flowers, landscapes, seascapes and horses.

Nev Wheeler was Britain's longest serving headmaster. He loved going to both the Library Poetry Cafe and The Writers' Group for what, unfortunately turned out to be his short time in Retford.

Patricia Graham has been greatly encouraged by the Retford writers group, which she joined a year ago. Thinking that she wasn't very good at poetry, or writing in general, the welcome, good comments and constructive criticism from group members have enabled her to be more confident, and her comment of "This isn't very good but I'll read it anyway" has been eliminated.

Rachel Hilton is a long term member of the group, but had to move away and since been a 'virtual' member via the internet, occasionally posting from America.

Daniel Toyne has been a teacher of literature in Britain, Germany and Singapore. He loves the rigour of classic poetry and captures the concerns of the modern world in those many classic styles. He is a priest in the Greek Orthodox Church.

Cheryll Richardson is a retired teacher and has written simple poems and ditties all her life .Joining the 'Worshipful Company of Retford Writers and Poets' has encouraged her to up her game by learning and listening to others . 'Wonderful to be in the company of such talented people.'

John Holmes is an Honours Graduate in social sciences; former insurance claims adjuster; member of Crime Writers Association; distinction in freelance articles course with London School of Journalism. Author of 8 books: novels, non-fiction, short stories including *Lily Upshire is Winning; Mack Breaks the Case; Legacy and a Gun.*

Barrie Purnell is a retired engineer who started writing poetry in his 70's when he joined the writers group in 2015. Since then he has published 3 books of poetry: *Poetry of Love, Life and Loss, Barrie's Ballads and Miscellaneous Musings* and *Holding On.*

Kevin Murphy has been a Friar, Teacher and Youth Worker. Wanting to write his own stories, he joined others in 2011 to aspire to be better at it. He is a School Governor overseeing Literacy and Sex and Relationship Education, he has found lots of inspiration, and continues to practice to improve. Published under the pseudonym Kevan Pooler are *Barred?* a crime mystery set in Youth Service; and *Convicted for Courage* a social history of WW2 POW camps in UK.

Michael Keeble has attempted all sorts of writing including non-fiction and narrative rhyming poetry, but most of all he likes to write stories. As with all his writing, he does this for the pleasure of writing and the appreciation of the group (although he does say that becoming a million selling author would not go amiss).

Samantha Richardson is an ex primary school teacher who has written poetry for the last thirty years after studying English Literature at University. She recently joined Retford writers group and has plucked up the courage to allow her poetry a wider audience.

Chitose Uchida achieved a master in her native Japanese, but having settled in England for many years, she has been fascinated by the language and poetry. She enjoys melding the two approaches.

Printed in Great Britain
by Amazon